W9-AGK-593

"Should I say good morning...?" he asked quietly

"I'm sorry I made such a fool of myself last night. And I want to thank you for your kindness."

"Kindness." His lips curled around the word, giving it an ironic inflection. The blue eyes gently mocked the evasion it implied.

"Yes." Eden hurried on. "I should not have behaved as I did. I realize it would be hard for someone else to understand."

"You think I don't understand what you felt, Eden?" he interrupted, his voice soft with knowledge. "You saw Marlee leaving with Ray. You had lost Jeff. A sense of loneliness closed in on you. You needed someone."

Tears pricked at her eyes. "Yes," she choked out.

"But, Eden," he added softly, "that doesn't answer everything that happened between us."

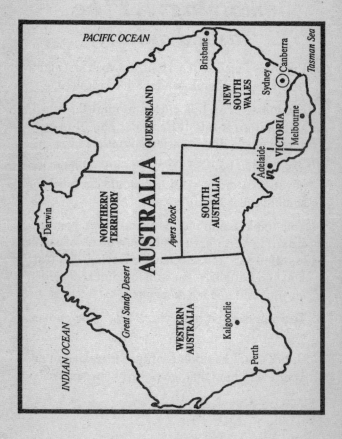

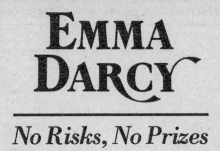

EMMA DARCY

No Risks, No Prizes

Harlequin Books

TORONTO • NEW YORK • LONDON
AMSTERDAM • PARIS • SYDNEY • HAMBURG
STOCKHOLM • ATHENS • TOKYO • MILAN
MADRID • WARSAW • BUDAPEST • AUCKLAND

If you purchased this book without a cover you should be aware
that this book is stolen property. It was reported as "unsold and
destroyed" to the publisher, and neither the author nor the
publisher has received any payment for this "stripped book."

Harlequin Presents first edition July 1993
ISBN 0-373-11570-9

NO RISKS, NO PRIZES

Copyright © 1993 by Emma Darcy. All rights reserved.
Except for use in any review, the reproduction or utilization
of this work in whole or in part in any form by any electronic,
mechanical or other means, now known or hereafter invented,
including xerography, photocopying and recording, or in any
information storage or retrieval system, is forbidden without
the permission of the publisher, Harlequin Enterprises Limited,
225 Duncan Mill Road, Don Mills, Ontario, Canada M3B 3K9.

All the characters in this book have no existence outside the
imagination of the author and have no relation whatsoever to
anyone bearing the same name or names. They are not even
distantly inspired by any individual known or unknown to the
author, and all incidents are pure invention.

® are Trademarks registered in the United States Patent and
Trademark Office and in other countries.

Printed in U.S.A.

CHAPTER ONE

FOR A PERFECT garden wedding, the weather had to be perfect. If the forecasters had it right, tomorrow would be fine and sunny. Of course, there were contingency plans to move the ceremony into the house if it rained, but that wouldn't be nearly so romantic as being married under the rose bower on the northern lawn with all the surrounding flowerbeds ablaze with spring blooms.

Let it come true, Eden fiercely willed as she lay in bed waiting for sleep to claim her. If anyone deserved to have her dream wedding, it was her nearest and dearest friend, Marlee.

Eight years had passed since they had both used the comfortless bunks in the St. Bernard's Home for Children for the last time. That was a long, long way from the designer-decorated guest room she occupied tonight in the Harcourts' luxurious double-storey home. She and Marlee were both twenty-four now, and the future they had hoped and wished for was shaping up very nicely.

It had been a good plan, becoming nannies. Helping to take care of the little ones at the home had given Eden the idea, as well as giving them plenty of experience at handling even the most difficult children. They could do it—that was the main point—without having to spend a lot of money on getting qualifications. Even better, it was a means of getting them out of the poverty-stricken life neither of them ever wanted to go back to.

Eden grinned as she remembered tutoring Marlee to speak nicely, to copy the speech of the welfare officers and teachers, not the slovenly language bandied around the home. If they wanted to be accepted into really nice places, they had to speak and behave as though they belonged there.

Which had also meant poring over library books on etiquette. They were not going to be disadvantaged if Eden could help it. Marlee, of course, had good-naturedly applied herself to all Eden's directions on these points, and the determination and discipline had paid off for both of them.

Not only had they gained positions in beautiful homes, but both had experienced a side of life they might never have known in another type of job. They had travelled overseas with their "families" and been given opportunities to see marvellous things and meet an amazing variety of people.

Marlee had fallen on her feet with the Harcourts. She had been with them almost five years, helping Pam Harcourt with the twins, who were so excited about being flower girls tomorrow. Marlee would be even more one of the family after the wedding. Pam's younger brother, Ray, was certainly intent on that. He and Marlee were so much in love they would undoubtedly make the happiest bride and groom imaginable.

The thought of the man Eden had to partner tomorrow momentarily dimmed the pleasure of anticipation. It was only natural that Ray had chosen his older brother to be his best man. She herself was as close to a sister as Marlee would ever have, so the arrangement of the wedding party had probably been a foregone conclusion—Marlee and Ray, Eden and Luke, and Pam's twins as flower girls. All the same, Eden wished Ray had asked a friend instead of his brother.

Luke Selby seemed to get under Eden's skin. There was a touch of dry mockery in his voice and a hard cynicism in his eyes that said he would never take any woman seriously. Certainly not Eden. Apart from which, he was too handsome for his own good. Although handsome wasn't the right word for it. More like animal magnetism. Knowingly or unknowingly, he threw out a challenge to women—come and get me if you can—yet projected an indifference that said he was ungettable.

Eden frowned over her reaction to him. He offended her sense of self-worth. That's what it was, she decided. She felt he only looked at her as a possible body, not as a worthwhile person. Quite simply, she preferred to keep out of his company, but tomorrow she had to do her best to grin and bear it.

At least she would have Jeff to escape to whenever she could. Eden's frown cleared to a happy smile. Tomorrow she would be Marlee's bridesmaid, but the next wedding would be her own.

Three more months. That was all she had to wait. Jeff had promised they would get the engagement ring and order a wedding ring to match as soon as he got back from Perth. Which meant one day next week, since he was arriving tomorrow in time for Marlee's wedding.

She had missed him terribly these past six weeks. The computer programming contract that had taken him to Perth was supposed to have been for three weeks, but it had dragged on and on with one snag after another. It had looked like he would miss the wedding, although Jeff had assured her he was putting in a superhuman effort to get back in time. There were some things, apparently, he had to tie up. He had done precisely that.

Eden sighed with satisfaction. Perth and Sydney were on the opposite sides of Australia, the huge distance making it an expensive business to even telephone each other. However, they would never be parted again. Next time Jeff had to travel somewhere on a job, she would be going with him . . . as his wife.

"Wake up, Eden!"

Marlee's voice pierced her slumber, and a shake of her shoulder brought her to alert consciousness. She opened her eyes to a face beaming intense happiness down at her. It was a soft feminine endearing face, but not beautiful or strikingly attractive. To Eden it had always radiated an inner goodness that soothed her own dark turbulent soul. Marlee was beautiful inside. Eden cherished her for that.

She was still in her nightie, but had donned a robe as well, obviously too excited to dress before racing into Eden's room to share the good news. "It's a perfect morning! Not a cloud in the sky! Come and look, Eden!"

Marlee raced over to the window to drink in beautiful blue sky again. Eden clambered out of bed and happily joined her there, sharing her friend's buoyant spirits. It was indeed a sparkling morning, heralding a sparkling day.

"I'm so lucky I can hardly believe it!" Marlee hugged herself ecstatically.

Eden hugged her slightly built friend, as well, affectionately resting her cheek against the silky brown hair that always felt as soft as a baby's. "The sun had to shine. I commanded it to," she said huskily, fighting back a sudden well of tears.

Marlee laughed and tilted her head up, her lovely amber eyes shining with warmth and appreciation. "Still looking after me, Eden?"

"Only for today. Ray takes over at four o'clock this afternoon," she said with a smile.

Despite her effort to keep the moment light, the knowledge flashed between them that today was not only the beginning of something new and beautiful, it was also the end of something that had sustained both of them in so many different ways.

"How do I thank you for all you've done for me?" Tears swam into Marlee's eyes.

"Marlee, without you in that dreadful home, I would have died inside. You brought to me the gift of caring. How do I thank you for that?" Eden answered softly.

They looked at each other, sharing the memory of a hard, rebellious, street-wise Eden and a vulnerable little Marlee who was a natural victim in the gentleness of her nature. Eden had protected her and taught her how to protect herself, and a bond was born that would never be broken, no matter what life dealt out to them. Today another bond would supersede it. Which was how it should be with marriage. They both acknowledged that truth as the natural order of things.

"You'll soon have Jeff," Marlee said.

"Yes," Eden agreed.

Although there was one small fly in the ointment, which they both knew and tried their best to ignore. Ray and Jeff were never going to be bosom buddies. In some ways they were as different as chalk and cheese. Eden guessed outsiders saw herself and Marlee the same way.

Perhaps it was the truth. Circumstances had driven two twelve-year-old girls together, need answering need, but their basic natures were hardly a perfect match. In essentials Marlee and Eden were opposites. Perhaps that was why they had found it so easy to share so much, complementing each other's strengths and weaknesses.

It was now all too possible their separate marriages would drive them apart. And so there was a sadness mixed up in today's happiness. Yet neither could choose differently. They had to be true to themselves and to their separate destinies.

"Eden, you will come to visit?" There was a crease of anxiety between Marlee's eyes as she searched her friend's for assurance. "Our friendship will endure, won't it?"

"Of course it will," Eden declared without hesitation. "No matter how often we part, nor how long we're separated, it will always be the same between us, Marlee."

Relief swept away concern. "Of course you're right, Eden. You always are."

Eden laughed and hugged her friend again. "Well, I was right about Ray. He's going to make you a great husband."

Serious, solid Ray—only two years older than Marlee but firmly set on getting what he wanted out of life. A career in accountancy, a woman like Marlee who wanted nothing more than to devote herself to her husband and family, a fine home, stability and security. Eden had no doubt they would forge a happy future together.

"And Jeff?" Marlee asked on a note of uncertainty. "Are you as sure about him, Eden?"

"He's right for me," she affirmed, although she hadn't been quite sure of that until she had let Jeff make love to her.

His tenderness as a lover had been the turning point. He was bright and clever and ambitious, and she admired those qualities. She had been strongly attracted to his blond good looks and confident manner. But it was his patience with her that had won her in the end.

She could never, would never, have a relationship with a man who took without caring or tenderness. She remembered the brutal animal her mother had lived with too vividly to ever allow a man like that anywhere near her. Marlee didn't know about the horrors that had driven Eden to run away from home. Although she could probably guess at the truth, because Eden had fought so fiercely never to be taken back. It wasn't something Eden would ever tell anyone. Not Marlee, not even Jeff.

It had been so wonderful that Jeff had valued her virginity. Eden was not going to spoil how special that had been by revealing the ugly ravagement of her mind and soul that had stolen innocence from her childhood. A smile of satisfaction curled her lips. She had saved Marlee from experiencing that kind of ugliness. There had been gutter-minded boys at the home from time to time, but Eden had dealt with them. Marlee's sense of goodness had never been tarnished.

The sound of a powerful car entering the gravel driveway drew their attention to the window. The dark green Jaguar SL was typical of its owner, Eden thought. Luke Selby was rich, powerful, sophisticated and a performer on any road at all. For Marlee's sake, she had to be polite to him, but Eden knew that Ray's older brother was inevitably going to spoil part of this day for her. It was the nature of the man.

"Here's Luke," Marlee cried, a warm pleasure in her voice. "He's giving us the most marvellous wedding present, Eden."

"You mean paying for all the drinks at the reception?" she commented dryly. Luke Selby wouldn't care to have anything less than the best served at any social occasion he was connected with.

"No." Marlee's eyes danced excitement. "I mean, yes. He's doing that, too. But he's also offered to finance Ray and me into a house when we find one we like. At interest rates we can afford. It's fantastic."

These days it was certainly not an offer to be scoffed at. Eden had to concede it was very generous, although a sour little voice whispered such an arrangement would hardly hurt a merchant banker with the money-managing skill Luke Selby was reputed to have. Nevertheless she injected the appropriate enthusiasm into her voice.

"That's wonderful, Marlee!"

"Luke is so kind!" She leaned on the windowsill, eager to greet her future brother-in-law when he emerged from his car. "It's such a shame he's never found a woman he's wanted to share his life with."

Luke Selby was attractive and powerful enough to get any woman he wanted. It was Eden's strong impression he chose not to share his life with one. Which didn't, of course, preclude sharing some casual pleasure with those who wanted to accept what little he was prepared to give.

"I don't think he's the marrying kind," she observed flatly.

"But he did marry once," Marlee argued good-naturedly, always inclined to give everyone the benefit of any doubt.

"And divorced within a year. Isn't that what you told me?"

"Yes. But you can't blame him for that. I'm sure there was a reason."

Eden had never discussed Luke Selby with Marlee. Marlee liked him. He was being kind and generous to her and Ray, and therefore Luke Selby could do no wrong. Except that was not the case, as Eden had heard from others.

"Yes. I suppose the poor girl who was his wife was lucky the marriage lasted a full year," Eden replied flippantly, then wished she had bitten down on her wayward tongue.

Marlee's eyes reflected the hurt. "I'm certain it wasn't Luke's fault," she said hesitantly, uncertainty clouding the confident joy of a moment ago. She looked wounded, and it was her wedding day, and Luke was the best man.

Eden grimaced an apology. "Sorry. That just slipped out. Of course you're right, Marlee. I'm sure if we heard his side of the matter, there'd be a very good reason."

Eden was rewarded by the flash of happiness in Marlee's eyes. She had said the right thing, but she didn't believe it. Her employers moved in the same social circle as Luke Selby. It was common knowledge he didn't even go to visit his own child from that brief aborted marriage. He simply wasn't interested. Apparently he had paid off any conscience he had with a huge divorce settlement.

Luke brought his car to a halt opposite the front steps. Eden noted he parked on the far side of the driveway so that closer access was left for florist and catering vans. It was hardly the greatest act of consideration she had ever seen, but it was something in his favour.

Perhaps she hadn't been completely fair in her judgement of him. He had certainly been very decent to Marlee. If she could keep that in the forefront of her mind for the duration of the wedding, Eden figured she could overlook the divorce and the fact he didn't like his own child.

She instinctively drew back from the bedroom window. In the spontaneity of her friend's excitement, she hadn't bothered donning a housecoat, as Marlee had, and although her cotton nightie was perfectly modest, Luke Selby always seemed to make her conscious of her body. That was another thing she didn't like.

Eden had often wished she had a figure like Marlee's. Other women might prefer her own lush femininity, but Eden considered it more a curse than a blessing. So many times it had caused serious trouble. If she hadn't developed so young... but that was water under the bridge. She was hardened now to male eyes stripping her naked, but she would have much preferred not to have it happen. People readily accepted Marlee as a person. Eden never had that advantage. She had a struggle to get anyone, particularly men, to see beyond her body.

Jeff did.

Eden felt that Luke Selby did not.

She heard the car door open and shut, and was tempted into looking over Marlee's shoulder, trying to see Luke Selby as a wronged husband. The image simply wouldn't fit. If anyone fitted the tag of a man in his prime, it was the man below them.

He was tall, with a physique that was confidently strong and masculine. He wore stone-washed jeans and a royal blue sports shirt that faithfully outlined the muscled breadth of his shoulders and back, powerful thighs that... Eden shook her head. Luke Selby gave women thoughts like that. Which was all wrong. He was just a sleek, strong animal who knew his capabilities and exploited every one of them.

There was nothing pretty-boy about his looks, but he had a face that commanded attention and interest. Hard planes and angles that gave the impression he had the endurance of a long-distance runner, but added up to a striking individuality that had to be called ruggedly handsome. The bedroom-blue eyes were a startling foil to his black hair and brows, and the provocative way he could curl his lips was a taunting challenge to anyone.

He had packed a lot of experience into his thirty-five years, and he exuded an impregnable and arrogant self-containment that could easily be intimidating if and when he chose to make it so. At the present moment he looked relaxed, as though he intended to enjoy his younger brother's wedding day.

"Luke!" Marlee called down. "You didn't let Ray's friends do anything dreadful, did you?" she demanded in a mock-threatening voice. "He'd better be all right. You promised me..."

He laughed, a low, throaty chuckle that seemed to slither down Eden's spine. "I assure you, Marlee, it was a very sedate night. Just a few drinks while we talked. I evicted everyone at midnight and tucked Ray into bed, as I promised. No hangover. He's every bit as bright as you are this morning."

Marlee laughed her delight. "Isn't it a beautiful day?"

"Absolutely dazzling," he drawled teasingly, his gaze sliding briefly, knowingly, past Marlee to Eden before returning to his almost sister-in-law. "Did you sleep well?"

They chatted on, completely at ease with each other. Eden made no effort to join in the conversation. Luke Selby made no effort to include her in it. But he was just as aware of her presence as she was of his. Eden knew that from the occasional flicked glance past Marlee's shoulder.

Did he see chalk and cheese, Eden wondered? Where Marlee's skin was a light golden tan, Eden's was pale cream. Where Marlee's colouring was light, Eden's was dark—black hair, black eyes, brows and lashes that needed no emphasis from make-up. Her full sensual lips were sharply delineated without any lipstick to define or enhance their shape. Her oval face and long graceful neck were framed by thick, lustrous hair, which hung loosely around her shoulders this morning.

Marlee was only a little over five feet and prettily petite in every way. Eden was a head taller, and as much as she craved being prettily petite, she was stuck with being statuesque and striking, although she did her best to minimise her physical impact, scraping her hair into a knot, shunning any make-up and mostly wearing jeans with extra large T-shirts hanging loosely to her thighs.

Nannies weren't expected to be fashionable. In fact, the more they blended into the background the better. A wife didn't want competition for her husband's attention, and Eden had had one or two problems in that area. Some men seemed to think that accessibility meant availability. Eden had straightened this misconception out in no uncertain terms, but it had meant leaving her job. She could not feel comfortable in a household where that happened, even after it was agreed it was a mistake.

She didn't feel comfortable in a household that held Luke Selby, either, but there was nothing she could do about that today. As Marlee's bridesmaid, she would paste a smile on her face and she wouldn't let anything Luke said or did wipe it off. After all, Jeff would be here this afternoon to make everything better.

"I think I can smell breakfast," Luke said finally. "I don't suppose you two girls have any appetite."

"Yes, we have!" Marlee declared. "Tell Pam we'll be down in fifteen minutes."

But it was Pam who came to fetch Eden barely ten minutes later.

"Eden, there's a phone call for you from Perth. I've switched it through to the study if you'd like to take it there."

"Yes. Thank you," Eden choked out, her heart twisting at the thought that Jeff might have missed his flight.

She raced ahead down the stairs as Pam Harcourt paused at Marlee's room to have a word with her. Eden knew the layout of the house, having been here to visit her friend many times. She whirled into the study, barely pausing to shut the door before darting to the desk to snatch up the telephone receiver.

"Jeff?" she asked breathlessly.

"Is that you, Eden?" His voice sounded stiff and strained.

"Yes. Is anything wrong?"

An uncertain clearing of his throat, then hesitantly, "Look, Eden...I don't know quite how to tell you this...."

"You can't come?" she wailed.

A deep sigh. "I'm sorry. There simply isn't any point. Not any more."

"No point?" she echoed disbelievingly.

"I've met a girl..."

Her heart sank. Oh, God! Why did it have to happen on this day of days! She couldn't bring herself to say anything.

"Eden?"

"Yes," she forced out.

"Are you still there?"

"Yes!"

"I don't know how to say this...."

Eden gripped the phone tighter. "Tell me," she demanded. She already had an inkling of what he was going to say. There was no warmth in her voice, but the one thing she prided herself on was facing up to and accepting the harsh realities of life. "Tell me," she demanded again.

He finally managed to blurt out the truth. "Eden...it wasn't only the job keeping me here. It makes me feel bad, telling you this over the phone. But it wouldn't be any easier telling you face to face. As for coming home for Marlee's wedding and pretending this hasn't happened...I couldn't do it to you, Eden. And the airfares back are so expensive. This girl I've met...her father's offered me a better position over here...and I've decided to take it..."

He went on and on, justifying his decision, telling her the marriage they had planned was better cancelled. They weren't really suited to each other...just sexual attraction on his part...and of course, she was sure to find someone else who was much better for her....

Her ears heard the words. Her mind soaked them in like blotting paper as she stood there in a state of shock.

In the end she had heard enough. Jeff was still mouthing self-serving platitudes when she put the receiver down. She looked at her left hand. No engagement ring. No wedding ring. They were supposed to have bought both of them this week. But that wasn't going to happen now.

She walked dazedly around the desk and sank onto the leather chair behind it. She fought off a dizzy feeling of unreality, ignored the sick emptiness in her stomach and tried to order her thoughts.

Jeff wasn't coming back to her. He wasn't going to marry her. Their relationship was over.

Finished.

Forever.

And today she had to dance at Marlee's wedding and pretend that she was blissfully happy and her own bright future had not just collapsed into ugly little pieces. Not love at all…no love for Eden. Sexual attraction. Which had obviously been satisfied when she had given herself to Jeff. No need to marry her. He had got what he wanted.

It was worse than her worst nightmares. Jeff had taken her in with his pretend love, wooing her affections with a long, orchestrated play of caring tenderness. For all that she had hated her mother's lover for his crudeness and cruelty, right at this moment she hated Jeff Southgate more.

But she couldn't afford to think about that. Not now. She had to block it out. This was Marlee's big day. There was nothing she would do to spoil it. If it damned well killed her, she would radiate happiness. She had to look happy, be happy for her friend.

Somehow she had to blithely deliver some excuse for Jeff's absence, make it seem unimportant and hide her bitter heartbreak. It was the only way of returning Marlee's gift to her...the gift of caring for another's happiness. That mattered more than anything else on this, Marlee's wedding day.

CHAPTER TWO

I MUSTN'T CRY. *I* MUSTN'T, Eden willed frantically.

"Will you, Ray Martin Selby, take this woman, Marlee Jane Richards, to be your lawful wedded wife, to have and to hold from this day forth, to love and cherish her..."

Eden blinked her eyes rapidly, afraid that once she allowed any welling of tears, she might not be able to stop a dam burst. She forced the necessary smile on her face, gritting her teeth hard against the emotional lump rising in her throat. She kept her gaze fastened on Marlee's radiant face as Ray made his vows to her in a deep voice that throbbed with commitment. *Think happy,* she commanded herself. *This is the real thing...for Marlee. What she has been waiting for all her life...*

The bride spoke her vows softly, but with no less feeling. Ray looked at her with glowing adoration. The real thing. *Store it up in your mind, Eden,* she told herself. *Never be fooled again. This is the look of love, the sound of love, the reality of love.*

Then Luke Selby stepped forward to hand over the gold wedding ring. Ray smiled at his big brother, then turned his smile to Marlee. Marlee smiled at him. Luke smiled at both of them. Then he turned and shared the smile with Eden, the first benevolent smile he had ever directed at her, and for some stupid reason it broke her iron control and the treacherous tears swam into her eyes.

She swallowed hard and blinked furiously. She dashed a finger across her stupidly disobedient eyes. She could feel the moisture clinging to her thick lashes, but at least she stopped any telltale drips down her cheeks. She took a few long, deep breaths as the marriage celebrant completed the ceremony.

"... I now pronounce you man and wife."

He started to usher Marlee and Ray over to the table where they were to sign the marriage certificate. Eden forced herself to move. It was time to link up with Luke Selby, to follow the bride and groom and act as witness to the signatures. The photographer was already getting into position to record the moment.

She didn't want to touch any man today, but she had a role to play, and play it she would, to the best of her ability. Out of the corner of her eye she saw Luke's arm come up, offering it to her.

She removed one hand from her posy of flowers, lifted it, slid it around his rock-steady forearm. She instantly suffered a heightened awareness of his strength, his masculinity. Luke Selby emanated an attractiveness that Eden didn't want to know about. She stared ahead, determined to shut it out.

Why were men the way they were? She would never understand Jeff's callous behaviour. Again the threat of tears. Furious blinking. Movement. Luke Selby reaching into his coat pocket, withdrawing a clean white handkerchief, offering it to her as they walked under the rose bower on their way to join Ray and Marlee at the table.

"While our backs are turned to the guests, give me the posy and you can wipe your eyes," he murmured.

"Thank you," she whispered, truly grateful for his timely consideration even though she couldn't like the man.

They affected the swap and Eden hastily mopped up the watery evidence that had spiked her lashes.

"Emotional things, weddings," Luke offered.

"Yes."

"Why do women cry at them?" he asked with a touch of dry mockery. "Men don't."

It helped Eden to pull herself together. She retrieved her posy and handed him the handkerchief. She flashed him a defiantly derisive look as she answered his question.

"Perhaps it's because they know it's the end of the beginning, and they hope like crazy that it's not the beginning of the end."

He arched one eyebrow in inquiring challenge. "You doubt there'll be a happy ever after for Marlee and Ray?"

"No."

"Then why cry?"

"They were tears of joy." She sounded defensive.

He flashed her an inquisitorial look. "Do you resent their happiness together?"

"Of course not! Marlee is so happy..."

"...that you cried."

"Is there something wrong with that?"

He shrugged. "Each to his own."

"Don't *you* think Marlee and Ray will be happy together?"

"Strangely enough, I do."

"But marriage didn't work for you."

A shutter of reserve iced his blue eyes but he answered in a tone of indifference. "A somewhat different case."

For a moment, the bitterness she had done her utmost to bury found voice with the same touch of dry mockery he had used on her. "What went wrong?"

The ice hardened. "It's none of your business."

Eden retreated, annoyed with herself for having been tempted into hitting at him. "You're right. It has nothing to do with me," she said dismissively. She was not interested in Luke Selby's private life, anyway. She turned her gaze to Ray and Marlee, who were at the table with the marriage celebrant.

"I want them to be happy," Luke said softly.

"So do I. More than anything else in the world." She flashed him a defiant look, conscious that she had spoken with more emotional fervour than she would usually reveal to anyone.

His smile was wryly whimsical. "At least we share that in common."

"We're unlikely to find anything else," Eden shot at him, before she remembered her resolution to remain studiously polite.

"Oh, I wouldn't say that." His eyes glittered knowingly at her. "Given the chance."

The chance to get her into his bed, he meant. That was all men seemed to want from her. An angry flush burnt into her pale cheeks, giving her a fine colour for the photographs with Marlee and Ray. Her black eyes were brilliant from their recent washing, and she dredged up a happy smile from some hitherto unknown depth of character and fixed it on her face.

The marriage certificate was signed and handed to the newly wedded couple. The soloist finished the bracket of songs to entertain the guests. Ray proudly wound his new wife's arm around his own and led her through the rose bower to present her to everyone.

The guests rose from the carefully arranged rows of chairs that formed an aisle of perfectly manicured lawn for the wedding procession. The bride and groom started moving forward, accepting the good wishes and congratulations showered from both sides and laughingly dodging some of the hail of rice and confetti.

Eden and Luke followed in step behind them, adjusting their progress to that of the happy couple who remained the focus of attention.

"Do you know I've never seen you in a dress before?" Luke remarked.

"What difference does it make?" She used a careless tone. Eden was resolved that Luke Selby would not get under her skin again no matter what he said or did.

He shrugged away her flippancy. "May I say it makes you look stunningly beautiful?"

It was her turn to shrug. "Who cares?"

"I do," he insisted, a charming warmth in his voice. "In your lilac gown, and your hair dressed in a cascade of ringlets, you look like a Southern belle. Very romantic."

Romantic? Eden barely refrained from giving a scornful snort. There wasn't a romantic bone in Luke Selby's body. She would lay bets on that. Silky charm. That's all it was. She gave him a mocking look.

"This was Marlee's choice, not mine. She wanted a romantic wedding and I would have worn whatever she chose to oblige her. On her behalf, I thank you for the compliment."

In actual fact, she did not feel at all comfortable in a Southern belle guise. Marlee had fallen in love with an old-fashioned crinoline wedding dress, and this mauve—lilac—costume was the appropriate bridesmaid accompaniment.

Frills and lace and bows and off-the-shoulder balloon sleeves and hooped skirts did not normally comprise Eden's personal style. Luke Selby was right about that. The bodice moulded her curves so tightly it could just about be an old-fashioned corset, and the low wide neckline was designed to focus attention on the full shapeliness of her breasts. The satin sash made a very feminine asset of her narrow waist, as well.

With the floral tiara of hyacinths and rosebuds and tiny daisies holding the massed ringlets of hair from her face, and the matching posy in her hands, Eden felt extremely self-conscious of her uncharacteristic appearance which had taken hours to effect, including most of the morning in a hairdressing salon. It would be a relief to wash her hair into its usual straightness again.

Above all, she didn't feel comfortable with Luke Selby's attention to the display she had to put on. She vehemently wished he would direct his bedroom-blue eyes elsewhere.

However, she reminded herself he had been civil about offering her his handkerchief so she bestowed on him a tightly polite smile, and said, "You look rather impressive yourself in a morning suit."

He gave a low chuckle. "Except you can't get far enough away from me."

She had separated herself from him as much as she could within a semblance of togetherness. Her hand barely curled around his arm. She had excused it to herself on the grounds that her wide skirts needed the room for easy movement, but that hadn't fooled Luke

Selby. Could others see her reluctance to be close to him?

"I'm sorry. I wasn't aware it was obvious," she apologized.

"It's not," he assured her. "It's very subtle. But it's there."

"Then it doesn't really matter." She wasn't going to pretend something she didn't feel, and she certainly wasn't going to encourage him to move closer.

There was a short silence.

Eden remained obdurate in keeping her nicely judged distance.

"Is it because I'm divorced?" Luke finally asked.

"Yes," she replied. That covered a multitude of sins.

Another pause.

Ahead of them Marlee and Ray had almost reached the end of the aisle and were halted by well-wishers. Eden was stuck standing still with Luke again.

"Divorced or not, I still find you attractive," he said.

Bitterness gorged her throat. Damn Jeff! If he were still going to marry her, if he were here as he was supposed to be, she could have got rid of this unwelcome attention from Luke Selby. It was all Jeff's fault that she had to put up with it.

She looked up at Luke Selby. She supposed she should be grateful he didn't dress himself in sheep's clothing, as Jeff had done. At least she knew where she was with this man. He wouldn't bother to dissemble. He would go directly after what he wanted. Without the frills of marriage! And that was certainly not going to happen to her now. How could she have been so stupid as to give Jeff everything he wanted....

Before she realised it was happening, tears welled into her eyes again ... and Luke was stepping closer to her.

"Allow me this time," he murmured, his handkerchief out and gently dabbing at her eyes.

"Be careful of my mascara," she choked out.

"I'm aware of the important things in life," he said dryly.

She stood there as impassive as a statue. Why was she letting him do this to her? She wasn't in control of herself, that was why. It was proving too much for her to handle—Marlee's wedding, Jeff's defection. And Luke Selby was being kind to her. Marlee had called him kind. Perhaps he was. He was certainly being kind and attentive to her at the present moment. She didn't have to read anything else into what he was doing.

Eden needed someone to be kind and attentive to her to fill the black emptiness she felt. Jeff was gone. Marlee was with Ray now. She had no—one. No one at all.

She looked up at Luke Selby again. He couldn't mean this kindness from the heart. It had to be a superficial courtesy. Consideration for appearance's sake. Yet he did have a certain softness—compassion?—in his eyes. It seemed to melt some of the hard core of bitterness inside her, made her feel . . .

She took a deep breath, fighting the silly weakness that made her feel vulnerable. It was crazy to imagine that Luke Selby might care about her. Even crazier to want it. He was not the kind of man she needed. Her emotions were running riot, and they had to be reined in. She had to be hard to survive in this hard world. Hadn't she learnt that lesson a long time ago? She took another deep breath.

"Steady on there. I don't want to poke your eye out."

"I'm happy now," she said grimly. "No more tears."

He stood back, looked at her intently. "So that's how you see me," he murmured, somewhat enigmatically.

She forced a smile. "I doubt that you can see what I see in you, Luke."

"Then tell me," he invited.

There was still that softness in his eyes, and all Eden's defensive instincts sprang to the fore. She came out fighting as she had fought all her life. Before she could stop it, her tongue impulsively ran away from her. "You're clever, calculating, self-assured, cynical, very controlled and manipulative."

It was the truth, anyway, she justified to herself, and no matter how attractive he was on the surface, she was not about to forget it.

His mouth quirked. "So that's how deeply you see into me."

"Which is more deeply than you see into me," she said tartly.

His eyes caught and held hers with serious intent. "From memory, this is the longest conversation we've ever had, Eden. If you don't allow me to reach towards you, to talk to you..."

"Talking is not what you have in mind when you look at me, Mr. Selby," she clipped out. Then, suddenly conscious that she had not been keeping up an appearance of amiable companionship for the benefit of onlookers, she fixed her smile.

"It's a beginning," he argued lightly.

"No. It's an end."

His eyes glittered their man-woman challenge straight into hers. "Don't you feel the chemistry between us? The interaction..."

She could not stop a hot rush of blood to her cheeks. "You're mad if you think that," she retorted, and wrenched her eyes from his.

"I'm mad if I don't think it," he said.

At that same moment, Pam's twins lost patience with the delay, broke from the procession behind Luke and Eden and ran forward to their dearly beloved nanny—who was so excitingly the bride of their uncle Ray today—demanding to be told how good they had been.

Marlee leaned down and hugged them. "You're the most perfect and beautiful flower girls in the world," she declared.

"Do we get our photos taken with you now, Marlee?" they pressed.

"Very soon. Perhaps you'd like to go over to the garden seat under the magnolia tree and wait for us there. We won't be long now."

"I'll go with them, Marlee," Eden quickly offered, then winked at her friend as she added, "just to make certain they keep their dresses clean."

Marlee laughed. "That might be a good idea."

It was, as far as Eden was concerned. It got her away from Luke Selby and the ideas he had about her. There was no doubt he had decided to take an interest in her today. Or pretend an interest for ulterior motives. As best man, he was stuck with her, just as much as she was stuck with him, and he seemed intent on making the *best* out of the situation. Eden detached her hand from his arm and stepped aside.

"Are you coming, too, Uncle Luke?" one of the twins piped up.

"I most certainly am. I want my photograph taken with the best flower girls in the world. You'd better save a place on that garden seat for me."

They giggled delightedly and shot off, darting around the guests who were crowding forward now that the formal procession had broken up. Eden tried to hide her exasperation at being thwarted in her purpose, but didn't quite succeed. When she flicked a hard look at Luke, he grinned, the unholy twinkle in his blue eyes telling her that he was perfectly aware of her evasive tactic, but there would be no getting rid of him that easily.

He took her arm more firmly and forged a way through the milling guests with the utmost charm and courtesy. Smooth, polished and hell-bent on having his own way. Eden silently added those items to her list of Luke Selby's dubious attributes as she concentrated her willpower on smiling at the people who greeted them with fulsome comments about the wedding ceremony. They were finally in the clear and trailing after the twins, who were already clambering onto the garden seat and striking poses.

Eden pointedly extracted her arm from Luke's hold. The formal proceedings were over, and she saw no reason for the familiarity to continue. "You're wasting your time with me, Luke," she told him bluntly.

He looked totally undeterred. "It's my time to waste." A self-satisfied little smile was lurking on his lips.

"I learnt not to play with wolves a long time ago. There's only one end to that, and I'm never going to invite it upon myself," Eden stated decisively.

"No risks, no prizes."

"I'm not a gambler."

"Perhaps not. But you're a fighter, Eden. Don't evade me. Fight me in the open."

She laughed in his face. "What spoils could I possibly win by fighting you?"

He gave her a whimsical smile. "Having an entertaining evening instead of a dull one."

"You don't want it to end there."

He shrugged, not bothering to deny her statement. "That's up to you. Men chase. Women choose."

The shadow of her childhood fell between them. "Not always," she muttered.

He frowned, then his expression swiftly lightened to an appealing smile. "I'm civilised."

Oddly enough, she believed him. For a man like Luke Selby there would be no conquest in forcing himself upon a woman. "Have you ever considered that I might not be?" she asked, her eyes taunting his assurance.

Blue eyes danced wickedly, inviting her to do her worst. "I shall defend myself as best I can."

He was, without a doubt, not worth another moment of her time, Eden thought. Today, however, evasion was impossible. She smiled at him, but there was no answering twinkle of wickedness in the blackness of her eyes.

"If you end up bleeding, don't say you weren't warned."

He was amused. "Danger is the only spice of life left to me."

Rejection and disillusionment were the only things left to Eden. She might bruise Luke Selby's ego a bit, but he was in no real danger. Not danger of life and limb, nor danger of having his heart and soul lacerated. Eden suspected he had closed his heart long ago, although he did show what seemed to be true affection for his brother and sister and nieces.

The twins were happily contesting how much of the garden seat they could cover with the wide skirts of their lilac dresses, which were similar to Eden's gown. The necklines were higher and the skirts slightly shorter, but they had the same frills and lace and bows. The same flowers in their dark curly hair.

They were very privileged children, Eden thought, and they had no concept of any other kind of life. Most probably, Luke Selby didn't, either. Not that she would wish the life she had known on anyone. She remembered the fear-edged anxiety that had haunted her earliest years and turned to look up at Luke, eyeing him curiously.

"I wonder how much you'd welcome danger if you were reduced to helplessness. Not for kicks. For real."

His expression changed to one of intense speculation. "Not even Marlee knows all the layers to you, does she, Eden?"

Eden wasn't sure about that. Marlee was surprisingly perceptive, and had often jolted her with the accuracy of her observations. Yet there were still the dark areas Eden kept hidden from everyone. She did her best to suppress them from herself.

"Marlee sees the good in people," she answered. "That's something I value very much."

"And you see the bad in people?"

"Yes."

"Yet everyone feels compelled to rise to Marlee's expectations," he observed.

"Even you?" she asked at him mockingly.

His eyes held hers, forcing a reappraisal of that ill-considered taunt. "Yes," he said. "Marlee's point of view is positive."

"It can also be blind. But I concede its merit." She gave him an ironic little smile. "As long as you keep your distance, no harm will come to you."

"I was thinking of something...more compatible. We could be good together, Eden."

Her eyes chilled over. "There's a price-tag for that, isn't there?"

"Why not consider it mutual satisfaction?"

"Because you'll never satisfy me."

He returned her ironic smile and shook his head. "There's not much a man can say to that."

The twins leapt excitedly off the garden seat, calling out to Marlee and Ray, who were now making their way towards them with the photographer in busy attendance. Eden smiled at her friend, who was glowing with a very special beauty today. She glanced up and caught Luke smiling at Marlee, too, as though he appreciated the picture she made as much as Eden did. Which didn't seem to accord with his way of life.

"Why haven't you married again, Luke?" she asked. "It's been ten years since your first brush with matrimony."

The blue eyes stabbed at her, suddenly hard and mocking. "Marriage or nothing, Eden? Is that your price-tag?"

"Old-fashioned of me, isn't it?" she mocked right back, her black eyes giving him no quarter.

He didn't come back with any clever retort. Or perhaps he remained silent because Marlee and Ray were close enough to hear and he was adjusting his manner for them. As Eden immediately did. They were on show again, not only to Ray and Marlee, but to the wedding guests who sipped champagne and were served little savory hors d'oeuvres while they chatted and watched the long photograph session.

The garden seat was only one of many locations the professional photographer had chosen, but to Eden's mind, it was the most romantic with the magnolia in full bloom behind them. They were grouped and re-grouped in a lot of different poses and in various combinations.

Some shots required Eden to lean against Luke with his arm around her waist. He comported himself like a gentleman, never once trying to press any advantage. There was no surreptitious squeeze or wandering hand. Yet she was very conscious of his closeness, conscious of the warmth of his touch and the hardness of his chest and thighs, conscious that physically they complemented each other, his tallness against her above-average height.

We could be good together... His insidious words nagged at her mind, even though she knew they weren't true. No more than all Jeff's persuasive words had been true. *Good together* was what Marlee and Ray had.

Eden's face started to ache from having to smile so much. Her heart started to ache, too, as they were moved around the garden. The Harcourts had a wonderfully well-planned garden. Feature shrubs and trees were mixed artistically with borders and flowerbeds. Having been brought up in the cramped terrace slums of Redfern, then housed in the welfare home, Eden dreamed of owning her own piece of land and creating the living and ever-changing beauty of a garden.

That dream had moved farther away with Jeff's call this morning. But one day, Eden promised herself. One day she would have it. It was a dream that didn't depend on anyone else.

Finally the photographer declared his satisfaction and they were free to move back towards the reception area. It was a relief to be able to relax. Eden no longer minded that Luke accompanied her. Even his brand of conversation was better than her miserable thoughts.

''Do I get a reward for keeping my distance?'' he asked teasingly.

She slid him a derisive look. "Your skin is still whole, isn't it?"

"Let's drink to that." He lifted two glasses of champagne off the tray of a passing waiter, then grinned at her as he handed one of them to her. "We have been far too serious, Eden. What we need is some bubble."

The last thing in the world she wanted at the present moment was to bubble, but she forced a laugh and lifted her glass in a mock toast to him. "To our separate futures."

"To our joint evening," he countered.

She raised her eyebrows. "Not giving up the chase?"

"How serious are you with Jeff?"

It was like a stab to the heart. "Not very," she said, turning her head away.

"He's not here."

They both knew that. Luke had known it since breakfast this morning when Marlee had asked Eden about the call from Perth. Perhaps it was then he had made up his mind to amuse himself with her. She smoothed an impassive mask over her face and turned to him. "So?"

"So I'm not giving up the chase. Not, at least, until you choose."

There was no choice. Jeff had rejected her. Luke Selby was no lifetime proposition. But he did offer her distraction from the pain she mustn't show, and there were still many hours to get through before Marlee and Ray departed for their honeymoon.

She summoned up another smile and clinked her glass against his. "To having fun then. At least until such time as the blood begins to flow."

The blue eyes twinkled warm appreciation. "Agreed."

They drank.

The champagne was fine. It helped. It made her feel happier for Marlee and Ray. It helped spread a numbness. It helped keep away the depression and the tears. Throughout the long evening, Eden drank a lot more of it. Having silly, frivolous fun with Luke Selby was diverting. It kept her mind off the serious things. She hardly thought of Jeff at all because she knew if she did she couldn't bear it. And after a while she felt no pain.

CHAPTER THREE

EDEN SWAM towards consciousness as though her head was filled with thick treacle. Some innate instinct told her not to move, to approach wakefulness with caution. Her eyes were glued shut. It was an effort to force them open so she left them closed.

Memories of last night started to filter through the murky mess normally called her brain. She stifled a little groan. She wouldn't have...she couldn't have... But the slight pressure on her shoulder did not reassure her. She must have. And if that was the case, it was time to put damage control into place.

She forced her eyes open to bright sunshine. It hurt. But the groan she didn't stifle was not caused by the light. Luke Selby was lying right next to her, his black hair mussed, a shadow on his jaw, one bare and powerfully muscled shoulder leading to an equally bare and well-muscled arm that lay hooked over the eiderdown. Mercifully the duvet covered the rest of him.

Eden shut her eyes again. Some memories she instantly shied away from, then forced herself to examine them in detail. Slowly and painfully she traced the sequence of events that had led to this result.

It was her own stupid fault. Luke Selby had not forced her to drink all that champagne. He had not had anything to do with her collapsing into a crying jag after Marlee and Ray had left the house to start their honeymoon. He had not forced her to spill out the history of her life. He had not forced her to tell him what had happened generally with Jeff. He had not forced her to do anything. On the contrary, he had been tender, concerned and caring. Very tender, very concerned, very caring. And that had ultimately been her undoing.

It had begun with her feeling grateful to him. He had whisked her out of sight of the other guests, up the stairs to the guestroom Pam had given her. She had been a mess—a hopeless, out-of-control mess—and Luke had saved her the embarrassment of being a mess in front of other people.

He had helped her out of the hooped petticoats so that she could crumple up on the bed. She remembered him gently removing the flowers from her hair, handing her tissues to blow her nose, mopping up the tears, bringing her a glass of water, saying soft sympathetic words. He had been absolutely wonderful to her.

When he would have left her so that she could undress and get into bed, it was she who had asked him—begged him—to stay with her, to hold her, not to leave her alone. Even then he had taken no advantage of her emotional weakness. She could not fault his behavior towards her. It had been . . . gentlemanly.

He had held her in a comforting embrace, stroking her hair and back with a soothing hand. She had rested her head on his shoulder and snuggled her face up against his neck. He had felt so warm and strong. He had given her the sense of being cocooned in a soft paradise of love.

How long he had held her like that, Eden couldn't remember. Eventually he had tried to put her from him, to gently urge her to bed and sleep. To her it had felt like another rejection, unacceptable. She had reacted with total madness. She realized that now, with burning shame, yet at the time it had all seemed very clear and logical.

She remembered him trying to reason with her, saying she was not in her right mind, saying—very tactfully—that he did not take advantage of women whose defenses were down from having had too much to drink. She had recklessly and passionately argued that she knew what she wanted and if he was honest he wanted it, too, so why in hell had he spent all this time with her if he hadn't meant to follow through on it, and she hated men who weren't honest.

She had goaded him into that first wild kiss. Then somehow everything had got out of control. And she hadn't wanted to stop what followed. She had wanted to lose herself in the feverish passion that had exploded between them. It had been nothing like she had experienced with Jeff. No gentle seduction of her senses. More like a blaze of primitive desires that utterly consumed her, turning her into a totally abandoned sentient creature whom Eden cringed from remembering.

She wasn't like that. How could she be? Yet the images in her mind taunted her with the truth. She had done those things. She had allowed, even encouraged Luke Selby to do those things to her. And she had revelled in every progression of intimacy, right to the climactic end of it. And when he had held her nestled against him, their naked bodies still humming contentedly with satiation, she had revelled in that, too.

Naked! Eden's eyes flew open again. She had forgotten about that. A little exploration revealed she was as naked as he was. And they were still in bed together.

If Luke woke up, he would naturally expect to reach out to her, to touch and . . . to start again!

Her stomach heaved. Her heart slammed around her chest. Very slowly, trying her utmost not to disturb the eiderdown around him, she eased herself to the side of the bed and slid her legs out. Her feet found the floor and she managed to lever herself upright without making a noise or any betraying movement that could wake Luke. He slept on.

For a moment, she stood there watching him. Not so much as a muscle twitched. Her eyes skated around the bedroom and found the chair where she had deposited the clothes she had worn yesterday morning. She silently crossed the thickly carpeted floor, scooped up the garments, let herself into the en suite bathroom and closed the door after her as quietly as she could.

She felt quite sick with relief to have a door between her and the naked man she had slept with last night. She shook her head at the enormity of her folly. The action made her feel she was on a Coney Island roller-coaster. Never again would she drink champagne!

She caught sight of herself in the mirror above the vanity and winced. Her hair was a mess of limp spirals. Her face was whiter than white. Her lips looked swollen. She couldn't bring herself to examine her eyes. She didn't want to see the knowledge in them. She stepped over to the shower and turned on the taps full pressure.

For a long time she simply stood under the pounding beat of the water. She didn't want to touch her body, didn't want to be reminded of *his* touch. Eventually she forced herself to pick up the bottle of shampoo from the shelf in the shower and started washing her hair. Having completed that task, she soaped the rest of her body, keeping her mind in a mechanical mode. The sooner it was done, the sooner she was dressed, the sooner she could make her exit from this appalling situation.

Her exit, however, required some thought. She considered various courses as she toweled herself dry and put on her clothes. Sneaking out without a word was tempting, but Eden decided it not only lacked dignity, but might prompt Luke to follow her to her employers' home to see if she was all right. After her exhibition last night, that was a possibility she couldn't overlook. Besides which, she couldn't count on Luke Selby staying asleep while she packed and left.

She brushed her teeth with vigour, washed her mouth out, then downed two glasses of water, trying to reduce the dehydration that was undoubtedly the after-effect of having imbibed too much alcohol. Or maybe it was the way he had kissed her, the way she had kissed him . . . it was little short of debauchery. Eden remembered her actions with a shudder of disgust. Luke certainly knew . . . But she wasn't going to think about that and she certainly wasn't going to remind him, either.

She grabbed her comb and started raking it through her wet hair as she concentrated her mind on exit modes once again. She had to speak to Luke, make it clear that it had been a one-night affair and keep the parting short and sweet. She winced. Hardly sweet. But she mustn't show any distress about it, nor carry on with any incriminations, which Luke didn't deserve. She had asked for what she had got, fool that she was!

Having reduced her hair to order and scraped it back from her face, Eden took a deep breath and forced her legs to take her out of the bathroom. Luke had not shifted. He was still asleep. Very quietly, Eden set about packing her things and tidying the bedroom.

The way their clothes of last night were strewn around the floor told their own story of mad passion. A flush of shame put color into Eden's pale cheeks. She hurriedly hung up the lilac gown, which Pam had offered to sell to a bridal-hire shop she knew, along with the flower girl dresses. Eden certainly didn't want to wear it again. She didn't want to look at it again. At least Marlee wouldn't be feeling the way she felt now. Marlee would be happy.

Eden hated touching Luke's clothes, but she made herself lay them neatly across the end of the bed. Better there than on the floor where they were too stark a reminder of last night's madness. Another horrific thought struck her.

Apart from any other consideration, what if she got pregnant? A frantic calculation didn't exactly sweep all doubt from her mind on that score, but she hoped it would be all right. It should be all right, she assured herself. She wished now that she had gone on the pill as Jeff had suggested, but with him being away in Perth, she had let the issue slide.

Shock brought her to a standstill. It was the first time she had thought of Jeff since . . . since Luke had swept her hard against him for that initial kiss that had blown her mind. She waited for the pain to come flooding back. Somehow it didn't. Which seemed all wrong.

She had expected to hurt, and to hurt badly for the rest of her life. The bitterness of Jeff's betrayal was still there, but the dependence she had once felt on his love was gone. As with so many other things in her life, she had stood firmly on her two feet and coped alone.

Well...not quite. It was as if what had happened with Luke Selby last night had anaesthetised the wound of Jeff's defection. Or more likely, her mind was having to cope with too many shocks right at this moment. Feeling would undoubtedly return later when this situation was behind her.

She stepped over to the window where she and Marlee had stood together yesterday morning, the closest of friends whose lives were about to change—but not quite in the way Eden had anticipated. The sky was just as blue. No clouds. Eden had the craven wish to turn back the clock, but life didn't work that way.

She hoped Marlee was deliriously happy with Ray this morning, that the first night of their honeymoon had been everything it should have been. If Ray was as knowing a lover as his older brother... Eden clamped down on the thought. It didn't bear thinking about. Marlee would never be the same again.

How could she ever have imagined this outcome when she had watched Luke arrive yesterday morning? She remembered using Marlee as a shield so that he couldn't see much of her. Since then he had certainly seen all of her. Now she had to face him with that knowledge in his eyes.

She heard him shift. Her heart raced in agitation as she swung around from the window. His arm had stretched out to where she had lain beside him. His head suddenly jerked up from the pillow. The next instant he was swinging around, blue eyes wide awake and scanning the room for her.

He found her, of course. She wasn't trying to hide from him. But her heart was in her mouth and she couldn't speak any of the opening lines she had prepared. She felt impaled by the sharp blue eyes which were swiftly taking in her wet hair, her oversize T-shirt and jeans, and the distance they implied.

He hitched himself up into a sitting position. The duvet settled around his waist, thankfully keeping the essentials covered. He propped his knees up and leaned forward, resting his forearms on them in a relaxed, non-threatening pose. Eden kept her eyes fixed on his face. It was too disturbing to look at the expanse of bare chest with the little black curls just below his throat. It brought back memories that were all too vivid with him sitting like that.

"Should I say good morning... or are you feeling there's nothing good in it?" he asked quietly.

Eden swallowed hard and forced her lips to move, to shape the words her mind feverishly dictated. "I'm sorry I made such a fool of myself last night. And I want to thank you for your kindness."

"Kindness." His lips curled around the word, giving it an ironic inflexion. The blue eyes gently mocked the evasion it implied.

"Yes," Eden hurried on. "I should not have behaved as I did. I realize it would be hard for someone else to understand—"

"You think I don't understand what you felt, Eden?" he interrupted, his voice soft with knowledge. "You saw Marlee leaving with Ray. You had lost Jeff. A sense of loneliness closed in on you. You needed someone."

Tears pricked at her eyes. "Yes," she choked out, intensely grateful for his understanding, grateful that he was making it easy for her. He *was* kind.

"But, Eden," he added softly, "that doesn't answer everything that happened between us."

She shook her head. "I can't explain that, Luke. I don't want to... even understand it."

He gave her his wry, whimsical smile. "Far better not to. Far better just to let things happen."

It wasn't the answer she had hoped for. He was clearly suggesting that having gone so far with him, there was no reason for her to put an end to their...intimacy. Heat burned through Eden's whole body in a flood of embarrassment and humiliation. It was difficult to hold his gaze, but she knew it would be cowardly to look away.

"I don't want an affair with you, Luke," she told him bluntly. "Nothing more is going to happen."

"If that's what you want..." He shrugged indifferently.

"It's definitely what I want."

Last night was excusable, Eden told herself. Deliberate repetition was unthinkable. That would put her on the same level as her mother who had let herself be used by that—that beast of a man. Although Luke Selby certainly wasn't in the same category as *him*. In fact, Luke had proved himself to be very humane.

His mouth curled sardonically. "Like a black widow spider. No difference."

"What do you mean by *that*?"

"You take your partners, use them and then eat them for breakfast."

The flush in her cheeks reached searing heat. "You know that's ridiculous!"

He shrugged again. "This morning I definitely feel used. You took all I could give you, and now you want to cut me dead. How does that add up to you, Eden?"

"It's not like that," she argued.

"Tell me how it is then."

"Last night you were very kind to me...."

"I wanted to be."

"And you got your reward."

Blue ice stabbed at her. "Thank you."

There was a distance behind the words, an edge of bitter cynicism that laid an uncomfortable guilt on Eden. After all Luke had done for her, he didn't deserve to be cut dead. Nor could she view him as a callous womanizer any more. That wasn't right. If she faced the truth, last night he had been all the things she would love to have in a partner for life. But that was dreamland, not reality. The reality of Luke Selby's life spelled out that he wasn't looking for a lifetime partner.

"Where would it lead?" she asked, wanting to give him the benefit of the doubt.

The ice melted to a speculative gleam. "It's an interesting question, isn't it?"

Eden told herself she was a fool to even consider it. "Nowhere," she answered, more to herself than to him.

"I haven't made any promises," he said softly. "But then . . . neither have you."

"And I'm not going to." Promises were probably considered bad taste in his sophisticated world, Eden thought caustically.

"You need me."

"Like a hole in the head."

"To fill the loss in your life of having someone close to you. And don't tell me there isn't a deep need crying out for precisely that. It was what I was doing last night. You need someone to love you, Eden. At the present moment, I'm the best candidate."

Black eyes clashed with blue. "Then life looks pretty grim for me because you'll only love me as long it suits you," Eden replied tersely. "And then I'll be the one disposed of."

His eyes narrowed. His face ironed itself into an impassive expression. "The fact that I'm divorced still rankles?"

"The time in which you did it does."

"That's not something I can change."

Eden pulled herself up. Luke was right. One couldn't change the past. It was something you lived with and learnt from. Had he learnt bitter lessons from his brief marriage? Were his present attitudes a direct result of it, just as her attitudes had been forged from her life experiences? She had blamed him for the divorce but she had no hard evidence for making that judgement. Marlee could be right. Perhaps it hadn't been Luke's fault. He might have been as disillusioned as she had been with Jeff.

Last night they had simply been two people sharing together on a level that took in neither past nor future. No plan on either side. No promises. Just . . . being together. It had been good. No point in lying to herself. It had been very good for her. It must have been good for Luke, too, or he wouldn't be arguing with her. If she kept denying him, might she be turning her back on something she might never find again?

"Spend the day with me. I'll take you cruising on the harbour," he pressed persuasively, as though sensing she was weakening.

Eden was sorely tempted. Yet the reality was that neither he nor she was going to forget last night's intimacy, and it would be there between them all the time, ready to reignite at a look, a touch. She would inevitably end up in bed with him again. Which, of course, was what he wanted from her. Once the initial attraction wore off, that would be the end, the same as it was with Jeff. Eden had the strong feeling that having entered

Luke Selby's life the way she had, losing him would leave her in a worse mess than losing Jeff Southgate.

"I'm sorry," she blurted, black eyes begging forgiveness for trespassing on his kindness and generosity. "I can't. Thank you for looking after me last night, Luke."

It was difficult to read his expression. Disappointment, frustration, a bleak resignation. "Then thank you for my reward," he said with a touch of cynicism that hurt.

Time to leave him, her mind dictated, yet something within her warred with that edict for several moments. She had to force herself to wrench her eyes from his, to move, to collect her things, and walk towards the door. She felt his eyes following her but she steeled herself not to glance at him again. Hard common sense insisted there could be no happy future with Luke Selby.

She closed the bedroom door firmly behind her and headed downstairs, her legs moving mechanically to put the necessary distance between herself and any stupid temptation. She felt strangely numb. Probably because she didn't want to think about that scene with Luke. There was a lot she didn't want to think about.

She found Pam Harcourt in the large living room that opened out to the pool patio. It was where the reception dinner had taken place, and she was supervising a team of cleaners who were setting everything back to its usual order. Pam was a generous open-hearted woman, four years younger than Luke and four years older than Ray. Despite having carried the twins, she had a well-kept figure, and her lovely vivacious face was framed by a stylishly cut bob of dark hair. However, her usual vivacity faded when she saw Eden coming towards her.

She knows where Luke spent the night, Eden thought, *and there's no way I can excuse it. The only thing to do is ignore it, if she'll let me.* She took a deep breath and started talking before Pam could say anything.

"I'm sorry I deserted you so abruptly last night, Pam. All the champagne I'd been drinking went to my head rather suddenly. I should have been helping you, I know..."

"That's all right, Eden," Pam cut in dismissively, a cool reserve in her blue eyes. "There was nothing left for you to do after you saw Marlee off. I hope... Is there anything I can do for you? Some breakfast?"

Forced politeness. It was clear that Eden had slipped a long way in Pam Harcourt's eyes. Undoubtedly she thought that her high-flying brother was stooping far too low in his choice of bed mates, and to do it under her roof was highly unacceptable and highly unpalatable. It was probably a serious breach of good manners.

Eden could feel her cheeks burning again. "No, thank you, Pam. You've already done so much," she rushed on. "Thank you for all you've done for Marlee. And for your hospitality to me. I appreciate it more than I can say. If I could use the telephone in the study to ring for a taxi..."

"Of course. That might be best," Pam approved. "I guess we'll be seeing somewhat less of you in the future. Now that Marlee is married," she added pointedly.

Definite disapproval. The lesson was very clear. Nannies didn't misbehave themselves in Pam Harcourt's home. Not as flagrantly as Eden had. "I'm sorry..." Eden began.

"We won't refer to it again, Eden," Pam interrupted stiffly.

She probably thinks I'm a little gold-digger trying to get my claws into Luke. "Thank you, Pam," Eden said, and took her leave swiftly so that Marlee's new sister-in-law wasn't embarrassed any further.

As soon as she had called for a taxi to pick her up, Eden left the house and headed down the gravelled driveway to the street. The ten-minute wait was excruciating on her nerves. At last the taxi pulled up beside her and she hauled her bag into the back seat with her, not waiting for the driver to offer her any courtesy. She gave her employers' address and the car moved off. She relaxed into the seat and closed her eyes.

Thank God Marlee's wedding was over! It might have been wonderful for Marlee. For Eden it had been a total disaster.

CHAPTER FOUR

EDEN'S EMPLOYERS lived in Wahroonga, which was further from the city centre than St. Ives but not a long way from where the Harcourts lived. Wahroonga was a high-class, high-status suburb, established as such long before St. Ives developed into a fashionable address. Most of the streets were tree-lined, and the homes were mainly large and very impressive.

Best of all for Eden, the gardens around these homes were marvels of creative landscaping. It had never been a chore to her to take her younger charge, Nicky, out in the pram or the stroller for a walk in the fresh air. Walking anywhere around Wahroonga had always been a delight to her.

Sometimes when she returned home from these walks she would note down a particular display of flowers that went beautifully together, or sketch out a landscape arrangement that she particularly admired. She kept a special garden diary for this purpose. One day, when she had her own garden, she had a lot of plans she wanted to try.

However, there were no plans at all in Eden's mind as the taxi carried her away from the catastrophic events of the past twenty-four hours. The future was a total blank to her. She wanted the past to become a blank, as well. It took all her concentration to keep telling herself that none of it mattered anymore. Both Jeff

Southgate and Luke Selby were now out of her life and had to be forgotten.

She breathed a sigh of relief when the taxi pulled up at the address she had given the driver. She quickly paid the fare and got out, longing to close herself into her own private apartment at the back of her employers' home and shut the rest of the world out.

Her gaze flicked upwards as she stepped towards the gate. Her employers were both committed career people. John Stafford was a stockbroker, and his wife was the fashion designer, Paula Michaelson. Both of them came from "old money" and they lived in considerable style.

The huge two-storey home was on two acres of land that boasted a tennis court as well as a swimming pool. Behind these leisure facilities was a row of garages that housed a Rolls-Royce as well as a Range Rover, a family station wagon and two sports sedans. Above these were the living quarters for the couple who were employed as chauffeur/handyman and cook-housekeeper. A gardener and a cleaning-woman came two days a week. The Staffords ran a well-oiled household.

Eden took the side path that led around the house to the private entrance of her apartment. A tennis ball bounced into the shrubbery ahead of her. She had just reached her door when Paula Stafford strolled into sight, dressed in smart tennis gear and obviously intent on collecting the stray ball. Despite any exercise on the tennis court, her short auburn hair was impeccably groomed and her make-up perfect.

The fashion designer was in her early thirties, a small-boned woman with a feline quality about her that frequently rubbed Eden the wrong way. The Staffords had never treated her as one of the family, as Marlee had become with the Harcourts. To them she was only the nanny, not a friend. It was a social differentiation Eden was used to, although she didn't agree with it.

To her mind, a person's worth was not accurately reflected by the amount of wealth he or she had accrued. Nevertheless, she reluctantly accepted the fact that society worked along that principle, and on the Staffords' scale of how important people were, Eden didn't rank much above the very bottom. She was certainly more worthy than murderers, rapists, arsonists and other people who hit the daily news, but as far as Eden could see, not by very much.

If she hadn't met Jeff, she would not have stayed with this family as long as she had. Her relationship with him had made her relationship with her employers relatively unimportant. And her position here had suited her well enough since it had been close to Marlee. Up until now.

"Eden!" Paula exclaimed in surprise. "I thought you were going to be away for the whole weekend."

Eden managed a weak smile at her employer. "I felt too tired today to go anywhere, Mrs. Stafford. Weddings are rather exhausting."

"Oh, yes! The wedding." Cat-green eyes lit with amusement, and her tone of voice held an indulgent condescension. "I trust everything went off well?"

"Yes, thank you," Eden returned briefly.

"It must have been an experience for you, being partnered by Luke Selby."

Eden stared at her with flat black eyes, feeling a wave of intense dislike for the woman. "He was very nice to me," she replied, her voice clipped with cold pride. So nice that they had ended up sharing a bed, but she was not about to tell Paula Stafford that.

The high-fashion redhead laughed. "Luke certainly practises all the social graces when called upon to do so. No doubt he was in top form for his brother's wedding," she observed dryly.

Absolutely top form, Eden privately agreed, telling herself that Luke Selby was probably tarred with the same brush as the Staffords. She supposed he would only have been considering a private little affair with her. It was unlikely that he would have wanted her at his side when he mixed with his friends. A lowly nanny was hardly a suitable partner for a merchant banker of his qualifications. She had been absolutely right not to be tempted into any further association with him. That was a one-way alley that had "dead end" written all over it.

"Well, have a good rest, Eden," Paula added dismissively. "You do look rather washed out." Her eyes flicked derisively over Eden's damp hair and unattractive clothes before swinging to the shrubbery where the tennis ball had come to rest.

Eden quickly entered her apartment and only just controlled the impulse to slam the door behind her. Usually she let Paula Stafford's ingrained snobbery slide right over her head, but today it rankled. Badly. Especially coming on top of Pam Harcourt's cold dismissal.

Time for a change, Eden thought fiercely. She had been with the Staffords for two years, looking after their two young sons. It was two years too long, Eden suddenly decided. She had planned to give her notice once her engagement to Jeff was official. Just because Jeff had obviously found someone better suited than herself to help him as a partner on his way through life didn't mean she had to stick with what she had been doing.

Perhaps it was also time to bring her nanny career to an end and take another direction with her life. Life was changing for Marlee. Why not for her, as well?

She had been gathering other skills for a long time now. She had taught herself speed typing. She could operate a computer. One of the older boys in her last "family" had been a computer whiz. He had taught her a lot that she could easily brush up on if she signed up for a course. Even Jeff had been surprised at how well she understood his work.

She had money in the bank. She had been saving most of her wages for years. It might be worth her while to make an investment in a new career. It was something to think about, anyway. Although if she did that, there would also be the formidable cost of living expenses, which were horrendous in Sydney. She would never be able to afford to live as she did at the Staffords' home. She had to take that factor into consideration.

Luke Selby's words of yesterday drifted into her mind. *No risks, no prizes*. But it was all right for him to say that. He was unlikely to be reduced to poverty-line living and all that went with it. Life wasn't pretty at the bottom end of the scale.

Her apartment here was tastefully and comfortably furnished. It was a matter of professional pride to Paula Stafford to have everything in her home artistically coordinated, even the nanny's quarters. The colour scheme was terracotta and beige with smart accents in black and forest green.

Eden had added her own personal touch with her collection of pot-plants. Apart from them, all she owned were her clothes, her books, her stereo and her collection of favourite tapes. She didn't need anything else. A television had always been supplied by her employers.

The layout of the apartment was simple and economical, but Eden knew that such a place would command a higher rental than she could ever afford if she tried a different career. A kitchenette took up one wall of the living room. A bar served as a divider from the lounge. The bedroom was separate, with plenty of built-in cupboard space for Eden's belongings. A small bathroom led off the bedroom.

Not only did she have all this space to herself, she also had free use of the station wagon. Mostly she used it to drive the children anywhere they had to go, but she could take it for her nights or days off as long as it wasn't wanted for anything else.

Of course, the Staffords expected their pound of flesh in return. Eden had to accommodate them in the matter of working whatever hours their heavy business and social schedules demanded. When they went out at night, she had to sit in the playroom next to the boys' bedrooms until they returned. However, since she could watch television or videos there, it was no real hardship.

Nevertheless, it was definitely time for a change, one way or another, Eden affirmed to herself. She would start looking for other jobs, cost out what another career might mean to her. No need to rush into anything without taking a good hard look where it would lead. Right now she felt too drained to think about it any more.

She wasn't on duty again until seven o'clock tomorrow morning, so she had the rest of today to herself. She unpacked her things, made herself some brunch, turned the television on and settled down in front of it, determined to keep blocking out any depressing thoughts. Somehow she couldn't summon up much appetite or much interest in anything. The day passed very slowly.

She lay in bed that night wondering what it might have been like if she had spent the day with Luke Selby, cruising on the harbour. She kept telling herself to forget him, but that wasn't so easy. What they had done together came too vividly to mind. But she had done the right thing in walking away from him, she assured herself. Over and over again.

THE WEEK PASSED SLOWLY. Although she was kept busy with the Stafford children, Eden found herself getting more and more depressed about the loneliness of her life. She missed not being able to talk to Marlee on the telephone. She missed having dates with Jeff to look forward to. She thought far too much of what had happened with Luke Selby. She came to no conclusion at all about what she should do next, although dissatisfaction with her situation added to her depression.

On Friday she received a postcard from Marlee and had to fight back tears. It read, "Having a glorious time cruising around the Whitsunday Islands. Can recommend it to you and Jeff for your honeymoon. The Barrier Reef is fantastic. The weather perfect. Never been so happy in my life. You were absolutely right about Ray. He's a marvellous husband. Lots of love, Marlee."

Eden fiercely told herself she was happy for Marlee. She truly was. Yet somehow her friend's happiness made her feel . . . left out. Or perhaps it was the reference to the honeymoon she wouldn't have with Jeff. Whatever. No matter how hard Eden tried to count her blessings, they all seemed totally inadequate to make up for what was missing in her life.

The Staffords had no social engagement that night so Eden was off duty once the boys were settled into bed. She retired to her own apartment but found no joy there, either. What was the use of material comfort or even luxury if there was no-one to share it with? She wandered listlessly into the bedroom and flopped onto her bed. She felt like crying into the pillow but her inner misery went too deep for tears.

She heard the intercom buzz in the living room and dragged herself up again. The Staffords must have changed their minds about staying home this evening, she thought, and envied them their togetherness. She picked up the phone and tried to push herself into the right frame of mind to be obliging.

"Yes?" she said as lightly as she could.

Paula Michaelson's voice answered. "Eden, Luke Selby is on the line for you. I'm switching him through now." There was a sharp note of disapproval in the tone. Paula didn't like playing the servant to the nanny, even as far as switching a telephone call through to her.

There was a click, and before Eden could recover from the shock of that message, she heard Luke's voice in her ear.

"Eden?"

"Yes," she choked out.

A pause.

"Are you lonely?"

The question pierced straight through any defences she might have raised. "Yes," she answered on a roll of black depression.

"So am I," he said softly. "Have you had dinner?"

"Some." She'd had no appetite for food tonight.

"I'll pick you up. Say in half an hour. Even if you don't feel like eating anything, we could share a table at a restaurant. Have a glass of wine with me. Coffee. Whatever you like. Let's be company for each other, Eden. That's all I'm asking."

"That's all?"

"Yes."

She closed her eyes and wondered if she was mad to want to accept. "You mean that, Luke? Just talking company?" She could hear the shaky note of yearning in her voice.

"Yes. I mean it, Eden."

He sounded sincere. Luke Selby might be many things but he was definitely a gentleman, Eden reminded herself. He wouldn't do anything she didn't want him to do. *Men chase, women choose.* Luke was very civilised.

A stupid lump of emotion almost blocked her throat. It was probably a foolish thing to do, but somehow she didn't care about taking risks tonight. "I'd like that, Luke," she got out huskily.

"Could you be ready in about twenty minutes?" he pressed.

"If you don't mind me looking a mess, I can be."

A low chuckle. "I don't mind you looking a mess."

He hung up before she could find a retort. Eden replaced her receiver in slow bemusement. She took a deep breath. So it was mad to go out with Luke Selby! At least she wasn't going to be alone tonight. And that thought brought an instant lift of spirits.

She didn't have much time to get ready and she didn't want to look a mess. Not in the kind of restaurant Luke Selby might take her to. Her jeans and T-shirt wouldn't do at all. She raced into the bathroom, stripped off her clothes and had a quick shower while she considered what to wear.

A dress, she thought, remembering Luke's comment about how he liked seeing her in a dress. On the other hand, she didn't want to encourage him into thinking he could influence her. It might give him ideas beyond just talking company. It was going to be hard enough not letting those ideas into her own mind, without inviting them into his. She needed something dressy that didn't show up her femininity. The silk pants-suit, she decided.

It wasn't really silk, but the synthetic fabric looked and felt like silk and it didn't crush. The pants were black and wide-legged, fashioned in a mass of accordian pleats that made the garment almost look like a long skirt until she moved. The accompanying tunic skimmed her curves, leaving them nicely understated. It was black and orange, the floral print accented by the black Chinese collar and bands of black around the elbow-length sleeves.

Having dried herself from her shower, Eden quickly did her hair into a tidy topknot, cleaned her teeth, then dashed some orange lip gloss onto her lips. Five minutes later she was dressed and ready to go, a pretty beaded black bag hanging by its long gold chain over her shoulder, black strappy sandals on her feet. A glance at her bedside clock showed she had two minutes to spare. Best to meet Luke outside, she decided. It would save any complication with the Staffords. She wasn't sure Luke knew about her private entrance to the Stafford home.

She locked her apartment and walked down the path to the street. She was in the act of shutting the gate behind her when she saw Luke's Jaguar turning the corner and heading towards her. She raised an arm to signal her presence, and he brought the car to a halt beside her.

It was strange, but in her hurry to get ready in time, Eden hadn't considered the impact of actually seeing Luke Selby again. As he alighted from the car her heart gave an agitated skip, then set her pulse racing overtime. His face was cleanly shaven tonight, but it was still the face that had lain on a pillow next to her in bed. His body was encased in a three-piece business suit, yet that didn't diminish her memory of the powerful masculinity of his naked body.

He flashed her a smile across the bonnet of the car. "I'm impressed by your punctuality, but I didn't mean for you to be waiting in the street for me," he remarked lightly.

"I wanted to stop you from going to the front door and disturbing the Staffords," she explained, flushing at the thought of appearing overeager for his company. Was he looking at her and seeing memories, too?

A frown creased his brow as he rounded the car to her side. "Can't you use the front door, Eden?" he asked, clearly not liking what he heard.

Her flush deepened. She was all too aware of the class distinction between herself and the man approaching her. "No. At least, not for private purposes," she answered quickly. "I have my own entrance to my apartment at the back. But I didn't think you'd know where it was."

"Ah!" he said, apparently satisfied by this explanation. He smiled again as he opened the passenger door for her. The blue eyes held a warm pleasure, nothing more. "May I say you don't look at all like a mess to me?"

"I made an effort," she said dryly, relieved that she had done so, because his pinstripe navy-blue suit was class from shoulder to toe, not to mention the expensive white shirt and the red and navy silk tie.

Noticing her glance, he softly said, "It truly didn't matter to me, Eden. I simply wanted to be with you."

On the point of stepping into the car, she paused and looked at him, searching his eyes, wanting an answer that might soothe some of the inner turbulence his presence evoked. "Why?" she asked bluntly. "Why me, Luke?"

He paused, giving her question serious consideration. When he replied it was with a touch of diffidence that didn't expect complete understanding. "You don't pretend." His mouth curled sardonically. "If that makes any sense to you."

She nodded slowly, appreciating that his life probably demanded that he be clever, calculating, controlled and manipulative. She could understand the need for a change from having to think like that all the time. "But we're poles apart, Luke," she pointed out quietly.

"Opposite poles attract."

"So they can." She smiled. "Thanks for calling me."

"Friends for the night?" he appealed.

"At least not lonely."

A weird sense of intimacy pulsed between them, one that Eden didn't resent at all. It was as though they were both escaping from their real lives. Time out of time. And it was all right because it wasn't meant to lead anywhere. They could say anything they liked to each other, or nothing at all. It didn't matter. There was no purpose in the evening . . . except being together.

Luke took her to a restaurant in nearby Hornsby. They were led to a table for two in a corner, which lent them a certain amount of privacy in a dining room that was well patronised. The decor achieved a pleasant peach and mint-green coordination. The tables were not too crushed together and the chairs were comfortable. Tapes of Richard Clayderman were played as unobtrusive background music. The cuisine was French.

Eden decided she could manage the onion soup so that Luke wouldn't be eating alone. He ordered a full meal and a bottle of claret. With their orders taken, they relaxed in their chairs and eyed each other with a certain amount of curious interest. Intimate strangers, Eden thought whimsically, and wondered what really went on inside Luke Selby's head and heart.

"Do you resent being a woman, Eden?"

The question startled her. "What makes you think that?"

His mouth curved into a little half smile. "Oh, I've been thinking about you all week. You're a beautiful woman. Yet instead of capitilising on your assets, you seem determined on negating them."

"It avoids trouble," she stated simply.

He frowned. "You're not afraid of me, are you?"

"No." She gave him an ironic smile. "I do trust you not to jump on me."

"So who did?" he asked softly, the blue eyes luminous with curiosity. "How far back does it go, Eden?"

She sighed, reluctant to dredge around in the dark past. "No-one jumped on me, Luke. I saw what happens between men and women. I didn't let it happen to me."

"But what you saw . . . was it normal?"

"I don't know." She shrugged. "Whether it was or not, I wasn't going to allow it to happen to me."

He hesitated, the blue eyes gently probing. "You said you ran away from being a battered child. Was there more abuse involved, Eden?"

Eden shrank from answering that question. It touched on things she didn't like to remember. Yet she didn't want Luke to have the wrong idea about her. She took a deep breath and told him the truth.

"Not to me. To my mother there was. I begged her to leave—" She grimaced "—I suppose you'd call him her de facto husband, for want of a better name. He mistreated her so badly. In every way. But I think she didn't know how to cope alone. I helped her, looked after her, as much as I could. Then when I was twelve . . ."

Luke muttered something darkly.

Her black eyes defensively mocked the sympathy in his. "I matured young. And that drunken animal who used and abused my mother started eyeing me. I'd seen him in action too many times not to know what he had on his mind, and I knew there'd be no stopping him. So I ran away. I was picked up by the police and given into the care of the welfare people."

"There weren't any relatives for you to run to?"

"My mother had come from a broken home. Everyone had split up and gone their separate ways. She wasn't in touch with any of them. I was the result of a one-night stand with a university student. Mum didn't remember his name."

"And is your mother still alive?"

Eden shook her head. "About a year after I left she fell down the stairs and broke her neck. That was the official verdict, anyway."

"Did you question it?"

She gave him a derisive look. "Who gives any credence to the evidence of children? Better to wise up and look out for yourself."

He nodded. "And you looked after Marlee, too, didn't you?"

Eden heaved a deep sigh. "When her grandmother died, the welfare people brought Marlee to the home. She was a total innocent. Someone had to look out for her."

"Where were Marlee's parents?"

"God only knows!"

"So you appointed yourself as her protector."

"Marlee was a good kid. I guess—" Irony curled Eden's mouth "—she was like I wished I could have been."

A warm admiration glinted in his eyes. "Then there would have been two babes lost in the wood. Marlee was lucky to have your strength to lean on and learn from."

"She gave me a lot, too," Eden quickly argued.

"Yes. I know."

The wine was brought and poured. The onion soup was served immediately afterwards. The melted cheese on top was so burning hot that Eden had to wait awhile before tackling it. However, the soup was delicious and she enjoyed every mouthful.

"Good?" Luke asked, smiling at her empty plate.

"Very good. Do you come to this restaurant often?"

"I've been here a couple of times."

Eden wondered what kind of company he'd had on those occasions. He must be free of attachments at the moment, she thought, or he wouldn't be interested in her company. Or perhaps he didn't cultivate attachments at all. Maybe he only had the occasional convenient liaison.

A waiter removed their soup plates. Luke picked up his glass of wine, swirled the claret around in it, took a sip, then eyed her speculatively. "You've come quite a way from such a background, Eden. Was it your idea or Marlee's to become nannies?"

She smiled, secretly pleased by the accolade. "Mine."

"For Marlee's sake?"

"No. For us both."

"But you must know that *you* are capable of more than simply looking after children."

Her pleasure faded. "I happen to think looking after children is important, Luke."

"Is that what you intend, Eden? To look after someone else's children until you marry and have children of your own? And then look after them? Is that the sum total of your ambition?"

Her face tightened. Her black eyes blazed a fierce pride in her independence. "Not everyone has your opportunities, Luke. Other people simply have to do the best they can. And I'm a damned good nanny, so don't patronise me because of what I am!"

"I don't mean to," he retorted quickly. "It's a serious question. Do you *want* to be a nanny all your life?"

"No." The answer came automatically. She still hadn't made up her mind what to do, but the need for a change had taken root. She instinctively recoiled from the idea of being subservient to the Paula Michaelsons of this world for the rest of her life.

Satisfaction glinted in the blue eyes. "You mention opportunity. And I take your point. So if a fairy godmother gave you three wishes, what would you do, Eden?"

She relaxed into a laugh. "Can I make any wishes at all?"

He nodded. "Any wish you want."

"I would wish to share my life with someone who loved me just as I am, and who wanted to share his life with me."

Luke smiled. "No more loneliness."

"That's right."

"Next?"

"I'd wish for enough money so that both of us could live comfortably and do all the things that take our fancy. I wouldn't want to be obscenely wealthy, but I would like to know we would never run short, or be worried by the lack of it."

"And what do you fancy you'd spend your money on?" Luke asked curiously.

She grinned, sure that he wouldn't guess in a million years. "Enough land to create a beautiful garden around us."

She saw a flicker of surprise in his eyes, then a gleam of wry appreciation. "So you have an appreciation of beauty."

"Of course. Doesn't everyone?"

"Perhaps," he observed slowly. "Other women might say they fancy beautiful clothes or jewellery."

The waiter returned to the table with Luke's main course. There was a pause in the conversation until the vegetables were served and the waiter departed.

"Go on," Luke invited. "What is your third wish?"

Eden gave the matter serious consideration before replying. "For us both to remain in good health so that we can enjoy our life together."

"Fair enough," Luke approved.

Eden grinned at him, enjoying this game. "So what are your three wishes, Luke?"

The blue eyes twinkled at her. "Oh, about the same as yours."

"That's a lazy answer," she accused.

"Not really. Other people might have wanted fame, or success in their chosen career, or obscene wealth so that they could sit on the top of the pile. That's not what I want. Not anymore."

"You like being successful in your career."

"Yes, I do. But I am that already. I don't have to wish it."

"Well, what do you fancy doing?"

A flash of wickedness. "Ordering everyone out of this restaurant and making mad love to you on the table."

Heat flooded Eden's body and blazed from her cheeks. "That's not very nice, Luke."

His smile was more appealing than apologetic. "Sometimes I'm not very nice."

"You said tonight was just for talking," she reminded him tersely.

"I did. And it is. That doesn't mean I cán't have a wish, Eden."

She took a deep breath and released it slowly, trying to lower her inner temperature and reduce her pulse rate. Then she took a couple of sips of wine, hoping that might help, until she remembered what she'd done after drinking too much champagne.

She didn't want that to happen again. It was up to her to keep her mind focused on what she was doing or she'd be heading for disaster. She wished she didn't find Luke Selby quite so attractive. It made her want things she couldn't have. She put the glass of wine down firmly on the table, then twisted it around and around until she had gathered her composure.

By the time Luke had finished all he wanted of his meal, she was ready to meet his eyes again. "Was the food good?" she asked.

He gave her a lopsided smile. "If you want the truth, I didn't taste it."

"That's a waste of money," she chided.

"I can afford it."

"Lucky you," she said dryly.

He looked at her for several moments, a calculating gleam in his compelling blue eyes. Assessing her flippant comment, Eden thought. She regretted making it. He probably thought she was eaten up with envy, and that wasn't true. Most of the time she was quite content with what she had made of her life.

"I could give you one of your wishes, Eden," he said hesitantly, still watching her intently, weighing up her response, his eyes hard with purpose.

It unsettled Eden. "A beautiful garden?" she queried lightly.

"Enough money so you won't go short."

"I don't think I like the sound of it," she said dismissively, hoping to put him off the subject.

"I'm being totally unfair in even suggesting it," he persisted.

He wasn't going to be put off, Eden realised, and felt even more uncomfortable under his steady blue eyes. "Why?" she asked.

"Because it gives me what I want."

"That, at least, is honest."

"Yes."

"So what do you want?"

"I want you to come and live with me, Eden."

CHAPTER FIVE

EDEN COULDN'T believe her ears. She stared at Luke, absolutely dumbfounded. She hadn't fooled herself that he had put aside the idea of pursuing her, but the idea of him wanting them to actually live together had never entered her mind as even a remote possibility.

"I won't lie to you, and I won't give you any false hopes about where this might lead," he continued in a quiet, relentless voice. "I don't have marriage in mind. But as long as you stay with me, you'll have the economic freedom to do most things you want to do, and be whatever you want to be."

She recoiled from him in distaste. "You think you can buy me."

"No. I want to share with you. I want you to share with me. Just as you said in your first wish. And I can grant your second wish, as well. As for good health, I can't promise you that, but I've hardly had a day's sickness in my life. So I'm a good risk there, too."

She searched his eyes, found no flicker of disrespect or contempt for her, only a burning desire to convince her that he meant what he said.

"I want you in my life, Eden."

"Why?" She could comprehend his desire to make love with her again, but to want her sharing his life, side by side....

"I never stopped to ask why." He gave her his whimsical smile. "I saw you, I watched the way you walk, I heard you talk, and I said to myself, I want this woman in my life."

"That simple?" It seemed incredible to her.

"If you're a man it's that simple."

She shook her head, unable to take it in. Was he in love with her? Luke Selby in love with a lowly nanny? Or did he simply collect women he fancied to be live-in lovers until he tired of them?

"And if I'm not interested?" she asked, scarcely believing the depth of his desire for her.

"I'll be very disappointed."

"But you'll live through it."

"I guess I'd have to. If you give me no other choice."

He wouldn't exactly be devastated by her refusal, Eden thought. Nevertheless, she couldn't help feeling flattered that he had asked her. His offer was far more than she would ever have expected. In its own way it was a compliment. Of course, there was no future in it. It couldn't lead anywhere, with Luke Selby's attitudes.

On the other hand, if she was living with him, she wouldn't be lonely. She liked Luke Selby. She liked him very much. She liked his kindness and his generosity and his understanding. Her body responded to him. What he could make her feel when he held her and made love with her could not be ignored. She might never meet another man who could give her so much. In sharing his life, new horizons would open up for her. They would be sharing lots of other things together besides bed. Or would they?

"We don't have anything in common," she said slowly.

"We will, when I find them," he said with an indomitable air that dismissed all obstacles.

Eden laughed. Luke was so confident, so assured. He really believed he could climb any mountain. But how soon would it be before he started thinking she didn't fit into his life after all? That she was beneath him in more ways than one? Then how would she feel?

No, she wouldn't invite that disaster upon herself—being dismissed from his life as casually as he was inviting her into it. If he raised her to the heights, then it would lead to a very great fall, and that would hurt too much. However attractive she found Luke Selby, however attractive his offer was, it was only a whim to him. For her it was a side path, which would inevitably lead nowhere good.

"What do you say?" he asked softly.

"Thanks for the offer, Luke..."

"But the answer is no."

"I'm afraid so."

"Nothing I can do to change your mind?"

"I'm afraid there isn't."

He grimaced. "Where did I fail?"

Her mouth curled with irony. "I'm not sure you did. Perhaps I'm the failure."

"Why?"

"I've never seen my life in terms of being someone's mistress."

"Partner," he corrected with a frown.

"But I wouldn't be your partner, Luke," she said quietly. "A wife is a partner. You're asking me to be your mistress. Your friends would know what I was, and what I've been, and they'd look down their noses at me. I guess I've got too much pride to swallow that for the sake of all you could give me."

"My friends would accept you as the beautiful person you are," he argued.

"Eminently bedworthy?" she mocked.

His face went grim. "Anyone who didn't treat you with respect would be cut from my acquaintance," he said with a quiet ruthlessness that commanded belief.

It gave her pause for thought. "You want me that much, Luke?"

"Yes."

She shook her head, feeling dazed that he would put her ahead of all the other people who made up his life. "You amaze me," she murmured.

His mouth slowly tilted to a self-mocking little curl. "I amaze myself."

"But you never want to marry again."

His face tightened, and a cool reserve slid into his eyes. "I've been down that road, Eden. It cost me more than I care to remember. I won't take it again. Not for any woman."

"Not even for children?"

"Especially not for children."

"I see."

His mouth twisted. "I doubt it."

"Tell me then."

"No." The brief cynicism was swallowed by a mask of pride. "I'll give you all I can, but you have to take me as I am, Eden. I'm taking you as you are. That's the deal."

The waiter came to remove Luke's plate and ask if they would like to order sweets. Eden shook her head, too bemused and stirred to want to eat. She agreed to coffee and the waiter departed.

"Do you do all your deals as cold-bloodedly as this?" she asked.

Luke leaned forward intently, his eyes sharply probing hers. "I'm intent on not deceiving you, Eden. We're good together. You know it. And while you may believe that marriage guarantees love and security, let me tell you there are no guarantees in life. Most vows exchanged at the altar are an act of hypocrisy that no-one believes in any more. Promises mouthed, but not meant by either party. I won't be part of it."

"No risks, no prizes," Eden said gently.

"You've had a lot of doors shut in your face, Eden. My door is open. Why don't you come in for a while and see how you like it."

"And if I don't like it?" Eden asked, although she suspected she might like it too much.

"You can always walk out again."

"And what happens when you want me to go?"

"You'll be looked after until you find your feet somewhere else."

She supposed that was fair. He certainly wouldn't owe her any more than that. Eden doubted that she could keep Luke's interest, but she could have him for a while. Was that worth the hurt of being turned out of his life when the end came?

"You've got it all thought out. I guess you've done this kind of thing plenty of times," she said flatly.

"No. Never before."

She looked her surprise.

"You're the only woman I've invited to live with me." He reached across the table and took her hand in his. The blue eyes blazed into hers with purposeful intensity. "I want you as I've never wanted any other woman."

The warmth of his hand seemed to penetrate her bones, and she found her will melting. "You don't give up easily, do you, Luke?" she said shakily.

"No. Not on something as important as this." He flashed her an appealing smile. "I hope you're weakening."

She laughed out of sheer nervous tension. "I think if you had a case of champagne you might get through to me," she said flippantly, trying to hide the turmoil he stirred inside her with his touch, with his wanting her.

The waiter arrived with the coffee.

"Bring a case of the best champagne you have in stock," Luke instructed.

"No!" Eden protested. "Luke! For heaven's sake! I was only joking."

"I'm not."

She pulled her hand out of his and waved it in dismay. "Please . . . I don't want it."

He sighed and looked the waiter directly in the eye. "Forget that order. The lady doesn't want it."

The waiter grinned and poured the coffee.

Eden shook her head, feeling swamped with too many thoughts and feelings. "I think you're a monster," she said when the waiter had moved away. Then impulsively, curiously, she asked, "Do you like yourself, Luke? Being you."

"It varies. Some times more than others." His eyes bored into hers, seeming to fix on her fluttering heart. "You're anything but a monster, Eden," he stated quietly.

She felt as if his hand was around her heart, gently squeezing it. "Please . . . let's talk of other things," she begged. "This idea is really quite ridiculous."

But the questioning look she gave him, trying to gauge the intensity of his feelings, gave her away. He shook his head, a little smile of satisfaction playing on his lips. Achievement glinted in his eyes as he read her mind for her.

"You don't want to be pressed into an immediate decision. That's all right, Eden. I'll give you a week to think about it. I've had all this week to make up my mind, so that makes it even."

"Thank you," she said, then laughed at the whole crazy thing. "I'll take a week to think about it. You'll probably change *your* mind by the end of that time."

His eyes twinkled their certainty that he had no intention of changing his mind. "Let's talk about gardens. Tell me what you like."

They talked gardens right up until Luke parked the Jaguar in the street alongside the Staffords' home. "I'll take you to your door," he said, swiftly exiting from the car.

Eden took a deep breath. This was always the sticky part, saying good-night, but Luke had assured her it would only be talking company. The problem was she wanted him to hold her and kiss her again to see if it felt the same. But she could hardly tell him that. After all, a kiss had been the start of what had happened last time, and she wasn't sure the same thing might not happen again.

He helped her out of the car, took her arm, opened the side gate for her, accompanied her down the path to her apartment. "When are you off duty?" he asked conversationally.

"Not until Monday night. I had last weekend off for the wedding, so..."

"I'll come around Monday night."

"What for?"

"To see you. To be with you. Because I want to. Do you have any objection?"

"You said I had a week to think..."

"I promise I won't stop you thinking. I'll just help the process along."

"How?"

"By making myself indispensable."

"Is that fair?"

"I admitted I was unfair."

They reached her door. She unlocked it, opened it, switched on the living room light, then stiffly turned to him. "Thanks for this evening, Luke."

He wavered, as if in two minds. Then he stepped back, touched his fingers to his lips and blew her a kiss. "Keep thinking of me," he said, then turned and walked briskly down the path.

Eden was ridiculously disappointed that he'd kept his word. It gave her a sense of frustration that kept her awake a long time that night. It also made her face the truth. She did want Luke Selby. More, in fact, than she had ever wanted Jeff Southgate. Which was a very uncomfortable thought, because she didn't think Luke Selby loved her and she didn't think she loved him. Maybe she needed to rethink what love was all about.

The difficulty was that if she decided to go Luke Selby's way, she might end up very much in love with him. And she had absolutely no idea of how she would cope with *that*.

CHAPTER SIX

OVER THE WEEKEND Eden vacillated between telling herself she was crazy to contemplate Luke Selby's proposition, and asking herself whether it would matter if she did try his door for a while. Paula Michaelson confused the issue further when she made a comment about Luke's call.

"Was Mr. Selby calling about your friend's wedding?" she asked casually.

Eden got the impression that Paula was quite piqued at having been bypassed by Luke on the telephone. After all, Luke Selby was one of *her* friends. Why on earth should he be ringing the nanny? "No," Eden said briefly.

Paula looked expectantly at her, virtually demanding a proper answer. It was none of her employer's business what she did in her hours off, Eden thought resentfully, but a demon of pride urged her to say, "Luke wanted my company."

Paula's finely arched eyebrows disappeared under her fashionable fringe, then lowered to a disapproving frown. It was perfectly clear that, to her mind, Luke Selby should not be mixing with a nanny. Nor should a nanny have the temerity to get so far above herself as to try mixing it with the likes of Luke Selby.

So much for snobbery! Eden thought angrily. But it did raise more question marks about going to live with

Luke. It would certainly raise a lot of eyebrows. Like Pam Harcourt's. And what would Marlee think of her? She would be letting down the ideals and principles she had set for both of them. She really couldn't do it, and furthermore, she shouldn't see him again. He put wicked ideas into her head.

On the other hand, the door he was holding open to her seemed to increase in attractiveness. A different life, she thought. A taste of Luke's life. It would be a higher level of experience that might stand her in good stead when he finally shut the door on her. Why turn her back on it? It was the door to more opportunities, wasn't it? She was twenty-four. Plenty of years ahead of her to find someone to love and marry and have children with.

On a wave of determined common sense, she went to a chemist on Monday morning and armed herself with precautions against getting pregnant. It wasn't that she had made up her mind, but if she did, she couldn't afford slip-ups.

Her heart skittered madly when Luke arrived at her door that night. She looked up at him—tall, handsome, clothed in classy success, blue eyes zeroing in on her mind and heart with compelling power—and Eden knew she was in real trouble.

Her impatience during the day, waiting for the slow hours to pass, was sufficient indication that he was getting through to her. Now her tension was piano-wire tight, expecting, anticipating things she shouldn't want. She tried to relax.

"Look! No hands," he said softly.

Puzzled, Eden stared at him as he spread his hands in a wide-open gesture of unarmed friendliness, dropped a tantalisingly sweet kiss on her mouth, then smiled at her.

Common sense melted but a thread of sanity raised some defences. "You are a disruptive influence," she accused as she stepped back, denying him any encouragement.

His smile widened to a wicked grin. "That's good. I'm finding you very disruptive, too."

"On Monday nights I watch television."

"Fine! I'll watch television with you."

With a resigned sigh, Eden walked across the living room and turned the television off. "I guess if you'd wanted to watch TV you could have done it at home by yourself."

"I guess so," he replied cheerfully.

"So what do you want to do?"

"I want you to show me your favourite gardens."

"In the dark?"

"There's a full moon out."

She laughed out of sheer nervous reaction to the idea of being romanced by him under a full moon. "Are you really interested in gardens?"

"In your gardens, yes," he said firmly. "I'm interested in everything about you, Eden."

"Okay. You asked for it. Don't expect any more than gardens, Luke," she warned.

They went. They looked at gardens. They talked gardens. They debated the charm of various landscaping effects. They came back to Eden's apartment. Eden made coffee and a snack supper of grilled cheese on toast. Luke sat on one of the bar stools at the kitchen divider and they chatted about what they had seen. Their eyes spoke another language that neither put into words. The intimacy between them lay silently undiminished.

"Do you have tomorrow night off?" Luke asked as he finished his coffee.

"As far as I know. On Wednesday night the Staffords are going out...."

"But tomorrow night is free."

"Yes."

"I'll take you to see *42nd Street*."

She heaved a sigh but couldn't restrain a smile of anticipation. Tickets to stage shows were dreadfully expensive, and Jeff hadn't been as keen as she was on theatre productions, so he'd never taken her. On rare occasions she and Marlee had splurged and gone together, but the idea of going with Luke was all the more exciting somehow. Sharing together.

"You could ask me," she chided.

"Will you come?" he obliged, blue eyes dancing their anticipation.

"I think you've persuaded me."

He gave a low chuckle that seemed to feather down Eden's spine. "In that case, I'd best say good-night and let you get your sleep."

He went, lightly kissing her but not trying for too much. Eden had the definite impression that Luke was a very patient man, biding his time, playing a percentage game until she said yes to him. Then there would be no holds barred.

Luke didn't pressure her on Tuesday night, either. *42nd Street* was marvellous entertainment, and Luke was marvellous company. Eden was breathless when she finally called a halt to proceedings on the doorstep of her apartment. By then she was definitely of the opinion that Luke was skilfully guiding her into a deeper and deeper response to him. Which was both scary and intensely exciting.

"You're free Thursday night?" he asked in a low voice.

"Yes." It was a bare whisper.

He reached up and gently stroked her cheek. "I'll be here."

She covered the lingering feel of his touch with her hand as she watched him stride quickly down the path to the street. *I am in love with him,* she thought. It was stupid and self-destructive, but even now the thought of Luke Selby walking out of her life was close to unbearable. How was she going to manage the future?

The next morning Paula Michaelson was on the point of leaving for work when she turned on Eden with a waspish remark. "I trust you remember that John and I are going out tonight, Eden."

"Yes, Mrs. Stafford," Eden replied.

"I hope you'll be able to keep awake."

Which was obviously a reference to her two evenings with Luke. Neither night had been overly late. Eden had been in bed before midnight both times, although sleep hadn't precisely rushed upon her. Paula had never made any comment about Jeff's visits to Eden, and she was entitled to have visitors in her hours off. It was Luke who stuck in Paula's craw.

"I think I know my responsibilities, Mrs. Stafford," Eden said stiffly.

"I hope so," she retorted, clearly implying that Eden had undermined her confidence.

The unwarranted snipe made Eden's mind up about one thing. It was time to look for another job. She didn't want to be a nanny anymore.

Eden made a point of being very bright-eyed when the Staffords came home that night, despite the late hour of one o'clock in the morning. However, it didn't win any approval. Paula Michaelson glared at her as she said a terse good-night. Eden went to bed and thought about what to do with her life. She was still indecisive as to her best course for the future when she fell asleep.

One matter, however, was taken out of her hands the following afternoon. Paula Michaelson came home unusually early. It was only five o'clock when she swept into the kitchen where Eden was supervising the boys' tea. Nicky and Tim clamoured to greet their mother, who gave them a hug and ordered them back to the table.

"Mrs. Walker," she said to the cook, "would you mind keeping an eye on the boys while I have a private word with Eden?"

"Leave them to me, Mrs. Stafford," the cook answered obligingly.

"Eden, in the study please."

It was an order. A very imperious one. What now, Eden sourly wondered. She hoped it didn't mean the Staffords needed her to stay in tonight. Was that why Paula was home early? Or did she have another bee in her bonnet about Eden's supposed lack of appreciation of how a nanny should act?

Paula stalked into the study, straight around the massive oak desk, which stood in front of the window on the far wall. She left Eden to close the door after her. She sat down in the swivel leather chair behind the desk. She didn't invite Eden to sit down.

"I'll come straight to the point, Eden," she started in a clipped voice that was supposed to project authority. "John and I have talked it over, and we've decided to dispense with your services. You can only become a bad influence on our children."

"A bad influence?" Eden echoed in profound shock.

"I'm sure you know what I'm talking about," Paula snapped at her.

"No! No, I don't!" Eden protested, struggling to make sense out of the accusation.

"Last night John and I were at dinner with a friend who attended the wedding of your friend to Ray Selby. Your disappearance from the wedding reception with Luke Selby was noted, along with the fact that you were seen going into a bedroom together. Do you expect me to believe that his visits to you here are innocent?"

Eden shook her head in bewilderment. "What has this to do with my being a bad influence on the children? My private life is quite separate to my job as nanny. And I've always kept it separate."

"You are living under the same roof. I will not have them exposed to your indiscretions."

"How could they be *exposed,* as you call it?" Eden argued heatedly. "I'm nowhere near them when I'm off duty."

"It is a matter of judgement, Eden. Your *private* life is becoming too *public* an embarrassment for us to feel comfortable about you living in our household any longer. The matter is not up for discussion. I am terminating your employment here and now. Is that understood?"

"Yes. It's clearly understood, Mrs. Stafford," Eden bit out, her black eyes blazing with furious indignation. She could go to bed with as many Jeff Southgates as she liked, but let her take a lover from the ranks of the rich and the powerful and she was a scarlet woman who would corrupt innocent children.

"I believe a month's notice is usual. I will write you a cheque for the month's wages, but we would really prefer you to vacate the apartment this weekend. That will leave you free to look around for another job.''

And leave me without a roof over my head while I do it, Eden thought bitterly. It was so grossly unfair. She was being dismissed on social prejudice, not for any failure to do the job for which she had been employed.

Eden studied Paula Michaelson in grim, contemptuous silence as the cheque was written out. She was a small woman in every way—small-boned, small-featured, small-bodied, small-minded. She would be totally insignificant without her flair for fashion. The bright auburn hair was strikingly styled into an asymmetrical bob. The green birdlike eyes were exaggerated with skilful make-up. In fact, her face was a work of art, courtesy of cosmetics. And, of course, her clothes were always stunning. But inside she was mean-hearted, which placed her with the scum of the earth on Eden's scale of worthiness.

The cheque was ripped off and held out to Eden to come and get it. ''I'll write you out a reference tonight, Eden. You can collect it in the morning.''

''What kind of reference am I to expect from you, Mrs. Stafford?'' Eden asked, looking her straight in the eye.

''Under the circumstances, I will, of course, state the length of your employment here and say nothing more.''

The bitch!

''No need to do that, Mrs. Stafford,'' Eden said, a fierce pride stabbing colour into her cheeks and sparking her black eyes to brilliancy. Never had she been released from any post with such a lack of civility. It was insulting after the two years of creditable service she had put in in this home. ''I won't be requiring a reference from you," she added, barely keeping her rage out of her voice.

"I should think you'll need it," Paula Michaelson said tersely.

"No." Eden stepped forward and took the cheque, wishing she could afford to rip it up and throw the pieces in the woman's face. "Thank you," she said with icy dignity, then turned and walked out of the study, closing the door quietly behind her.

She went straight to her apartment and started packing. She was still seething over the scene with Paula Michaelson when Luke knocked on her door two hours later. She flung the door open, looked at the man who had been the cause of her dismissal without a decent reference, and vowed she would thumb her nose at every snotty high-class woman who crossed the new path she was about to take. Especially Paula Michaelson!

"Do you still want me to live with you, Luke?" she asked.

"Very definitely," he replied without hesitation and with heart-warming emphasis.

"And all the things you promised me last Friday night still hold good? You'll make everyone we mix with treat me with respect, or cut them from your acquaintance?"

"Yes," he said with satisfactory fervour.

"Will you take me with you now? Tonight?"

The blue eyes lit with triumph. "Right this minute, if you're ready, Eden."

"I'm not finished packing yet."

"Tell me what to do and I'll help."

Eden stood back and waved him inside. "You could take these boxes of books out to your car, if you like.

And the tape deck. And this suitcase. All I've got to do is shower and change my clothes, and then we can go."

"Right! Go and have your shower. I'll have this cleared by the time you come out."

He hefted a box of books in his arms and took off out the door, not the least bit inclined to question her decision and only too ready to implement it at all speed. Which suited Eden just fine.

She took a long shower, soaping her body all over, extremely conscious of what Luke expected of their living together. She hoped he had some champagne at home, because she had an awful suspicion she was going to be an emotional and nervous mess when it came to the crunch. What she was going to have to do was something she had very little practice at.

She washed her long hair, squeezed the excess moisture from it, then turned off the taps and towelled herself dry. Remembering Luke's comment about her negating her assets instead of capitilising on them, she blow-dried the thick black tresses into gleaming softness and curled the ends around her shoulders.

She dressed in the orange and black pants-suit she had worn the previous Friday night. It might not be overtly sexy but it was the most sophisticated outfit she owned, apart from an evening dress, which was inappropriate. She hesitated over wearing lipstick, then decided she might as well finish making the most of her appearance before Luke started kissing her.

Having prepared herself to face a new life, Eden zipped up her toilet bag, collected her discarded clothes and left the bathroom. She put these last things in her overnight bag, which she had set on her bed, closed the bag, picked it up, made a last check that she had not left anything behind, then carried her bag to the living-room.

Luke was sitting on one of the bar stools waiting for her. His eyes drank her in, glinting appreciation of her efforts to please him, but he made no comment. "I can't fit your pot-plants in the car, Eden," he said as he stood up. "I'll have a carrier collect them in the morning."

"Thanks, Luke," she said huskily. A lump had suddenly stuck in her throat. She was acting on the spur of the moment... *reacting* rather than following a carefully thought-out plan. Was she doing the right thing?

Doesn't matter, she told herself firmly. Decision made. No turning back now. This is the path forward. This is my commitment to a new and different future.

Luke stepped over and took the bag from her, then wrapped his hand possessively around hers. "Let's go," he said softly.

"Yes," she agreed.

He paused a moment, his eyes probing the flashing black brilliance of hers. "No regrets?"

"None at all," she declared.

"You're a brave girl, Eden."

"Or a fool," she retorted. "But I'd rather be a fool with you than not have you at all, Luke."

His mouth curved into a wry little smile of appreciation. "I guess that about sums it up for me, too."

They walked out of the apartment together. Eden closed the door on it. Another door was opening for her. Where it led she did not know, but it was enough at this moment that Luke was holding her hand. *I'm not alone,* she thought. *He's at my side and we're going to share our lives. For a while, anyway.*

They walked to the street. Eden shut the gate behind them. She waited beside the car while Luke put her overnight bag into the boot.

"I guess Paula wasn't too happy about you leaving without proper notice," Luke commented dryly as he moved to open the passenger door for her.

"It was her choice. She dismissed me," Eden told him baldly.

It stopped him in the act of lifting the door handle. He straightened and turned to her, his face all hard planes, the blue eyes as sharp as lasers. "*She* dismissed *you*?" he repeated in a soft voice that somehow shrieked of dangerous undertones.

Eden's chin lifted in defiant pride. "It had nothing to do with how I did my job. I had turned into an embarrassment for her because of you, Luke. Nannies aren't supposed to be so indiscreet as to be seen associating intimately with a man like you."

"Is that so?" he said, his voice softer, lower, infinitely more dangerous.

"In such circumstances, I don't even warrant a decent reference for the job I've done," Eden said bitterly.

"You don't say."

"It's a fact of life."

"And is that the reason you're coming with me now?"

"I would have decided to do that anyway," she said hollowly.

"But this precipitated matters."

"Yes."

"Associating with me has been damaging."

"That's an understatement."

"Then let's fix it up."

He took Eden's arm, tucked it around his and set off towards the Staffords' home, hauling Eden with him.

"What are you doing?" Eden asked anxiously, her heart hammering in agitation over Luke's determination and what she had set in motion with her bitter words.

"I'm going to prove to you that I mean what I say," he bit out, his jaw clenched in tightly controlled anger.

His face had the hard-chiselled look of a matador ready to take up the fight. In his black trousers and white open-necked shirt, the image was almost perfect, Eden thought, except that he lacked a cape.

"You can't do anything about this!" she hissed at him as they mounted the steps that led to the front door. "It's done, Luke. Finished."

"You might be surprised at what I can do," he said grimly, then punched the button for the door chimes with an air of relentless and unyielding purpose.

"Please don't be angry!"

He turned to her, surprised. "This has got nothing to do with anger. This has to do with getting even," he stated decisively.

Eden said no more. While she did not expect the scene with Paula Michaelson to be pleasant, there was a dreadful fascination about what might happen. There was also a definite excitement about having a man fight a battle for you. It had never happened to Eden before. Apart from which, it would give her a good idea of what it was like to have Luke Selby as her lover.

CHAPTER SEVEN

JOHN STAFFORD opened the door. He was a short, stocky man with an amiable, well-fed face. His hair had receded to a semicircle around a bald pate, and he wore gold-rimmed glasses, which lent a certain distinction to his bland countenance. The eyes behind the glasses were a bright brown and projected a shrewd intelligence. He still wore his business suit, but his usual air of being on top of everything was shaken by seeing Luke and Eden together on his doorstep.

"Good evening, John," Luke greeted him, stretching his lips into a smile that had a sharklike quality about it.

"Luke," the stockbroker managed in reply.

"I'd like a word with Paula, if it wouldn't be too much trouble for her to see me. A matter of some business for her."

The stockbroker rallied to the cause. "Well...of course. Paula is always interested in business. Do come in, Luke..." He hesitated, then brought himself to acknowledge Eden as well. "And Eden."

"Thank you," Luke said, drawing Eden inside with him as John Stafford stepped back to give them entrance.

"We're having after-dinner coffee in the lounge," their host directed, ushering them through the foyer.

"You don't mind if we join you?" Luke asked, playing the polite game with skilful charm.

"Not at all," came the predictable answer.

Paula Michaelson's face froze in shock when she saw who the unexpected guests were. Score one for me, Eden thought with satisfaction.

"Luke," Paula choked out, rising from an elegant armchair without her usual studied grace. She swallowed hard, then made a creditable recovery, forcing out the polite formula. "How nice to see you!"

"Luke said he had some business to discuss with you, Paula," her husband put in quickly, signalling the correct responses to the situation.

A stiff smile. "Oh, really?" A hand jerked out in a gesture of invitation. "Please...come and sit down with us."

"Thank you, Paula," Luke said with another smile.

He escorted Eden to the brocade-covered sofa grouped with the armchairs where the Staffords had been settled. A tray of coffee things was on the low marble table between them. Eden had never sat in this room before. However, seated beside Luke, with her hand firmly enveloped in his, she found the experience particularly sweet.

"Can I offer you some coffee?" Paula asked in a somewhat strained voice.

Luke looked inquiringly at Eden. "Would you like coffee, Eden?"

"No, thank you. I don't feel like coffee," she replied.

Luke grinned at her, a very definite gleam of unholy purpose in his eyes. "Neither do I." He extended the grin to both the Staffords. "What we need is some champagne to celebrate. You wouldn't happen to have a bottle to hand, would you, John?"

"Certainly," he obliged. "If you'll tell us what you're celebrating."

"Eden has finally agreed to share her life with me. She's moving into my apartment tonight, and from now on we're going to be together," he proudly announced.

Eden saw Paula Michaelson's mouth drop open. Luke immediately turned to her, radiating spurious goodwill.

"And I want to thank you, Paula, for the great favour you've done me in releasing Eden from her employment with you at such short notice," he purred, like a tiger whose good mood could be nurtured by the correct stroking. "I realise it's a great loss to you," he continued, feeding Paula the words she was to repeat—or the claws would come out with a vengeance. "You couldn't have had a better nanny for your children, and I know how difficult it will be—quite impossible really—for you to replace her. After all, she has been an invaluable member of your household, virtually one of the family. So I felt the least I could do to compensate you was to place some profitable business your way."

"My God! What business?" Paula choked out.

"I'd like you to design a range of clothes for Eden. You know the kind of social life I lead, Paula, and naturally I want Eden at my side all the time from now on. I'm sure you can come up with brilliant designs that will enhance her unique beauty." He cast a caring look at Eden. "She's perfect to me just as she is, but I want her to have everything that will make her feel absolutely right with me."

Paula's throat moved in a convulsive swallow. "How much are you thinking of spending?"

"More than any other client has ever spent with you. An absolutely obscene amount of money," Luke drawled with relish.

Eden opened her mouth to protest such unnecessary extravagance, but Luke squeezed her hand hard and she held her tongue, realising that her present wardrobe was hopelessly inadequate for the life she would lead with Luke.

"I see," Paula murmured dazedly.

"You will realise that I want Eden to have everything she wants. With the amount of money involved, she must be the boss," Luke pushed on, driving home Eden's change of status.

Paula flinched. Her eyes flicked to Eden and then back to Luke. "How much did you say?"

"The sky is the limit."

"She's the boss," Paula said weakly, bewildered by this totally startling turn of events.

It was far too much for Eden to reasonably accept. "Luke, no," she protested. "You shouldn't spend—"

"My dear Eden," Paula broke in, her voice gathering strength. "Luke is absolutely right to see that you're fittingly dressed as his partner. And of course I will give you what you want."

"I knew you would see it my way, Paula." Luke smiled approval at her. "And I know you won't disappoint me. You can certainly give Eden what I want her to have. You truly are one of the most creative women of my acquaintance."

A flush brightened her powdered cheeks. "How kind of you to say so!" The green eyes were momentarily glazed as she looked at Eden, then sharpened to the reality of the situation. "John . . . the champagne?"

"Coming right up, darling," he chimed in on cue, and made a swift exit to supply the necessary oil for smoothing over what could have been extremely stormy waters.

Eden sat there silently evaluating and marvelling over what she had just witnessed. She remembered telling Luke he was clever, calculating, self-assured, cynical, very controlled and manipulative. What she had not appreciated was how those qualities could be wielded to such devastating effect. And on her behalf.

She began to understand why Luke thought he could climb any mountain he set his mind on. He certainly made a formidable adversary. Eden thought she would not like to be offside with him. Apparently Paula Stafford thought the same thing.

Eden had no doubt that Luke's story of the end of her nanny career would be the one repeated for public consumption from now on. Any report of her employment with the Staffords would be a glowing one. Damage control had been swiftly and effectively secured. Her new life with Luke had been put on a partner footing in Paula Michaelson's eyes, if not in Eden's. Respect was assured. The amount of money that Luke was prepared to spend on her to gain that respect boggled Eden's mind.

He smoothly moved into specific arrangements. "I thought I might take Eden into your establishment on Saturday morning to get some *pro tempore* clothes. Would you be free to join us there? Give us the benefit of your impeccable eye?"

"I'd be delighted to help, Luke," Paula replied, beginning to ooze charm. "And while you're there, we could look through fabrics and see what might meet Eden's requirements." She managed a smile at Eden. "I wouldn't like to design anything you mightn't be happy with."

"I've always admired your work," Eden said truthfully.

Paula forced a little laugh. "Then we shouldn't have any problems. You're tall enough to wear practically anything well, Eden. I'll enjoy designing for you."

"Thank you," Eden said, amazed at the total turnaround in attitude towards her. It was really rather contemptible that money could buy worthiness.

John Stafford returned with the champagne. Toasts were drunk. Good cheer was spread. With everything amicably settled and understood, both the Staffords accompanied Luke and Eden to the door to see them on their way.

Luke slid his arm around Eden's waist as they walked to the car. "Better now?" he murmured, smiling at her.

She laughed. "I revise my opinion. You're not a monster, Luke. You're a devil. But how did you know they would climb down?"

He chuckled. "The Staffords have a large overdraft at my bank. That gives me a lot of leeway. But one should never force without sweetening the pill. For the best result, a balance of respect has to be maintained."

Eden thought about that as Luke saw her settled into his car. She watched him round the bonnet to the driver's side, his step eager. A man who knew what he was doing. A man who knew what had to be done to accomplish what he wanted. A man who got what he wanted. He settled onto the seat beside her and closed his door. There was a look of deep satisfaction on his face.

"What strength did you think you had in dealing with me, Luke?" Eden asked. "Why did you think I'd give in?"

The blue eyes held absolute certainty as he answered. "Your response to me the night of Marlee's wedding."

Her smile was wry. "Under the influence of too much champagne?"

"*In vino, veritas,*" he softly quoted. "That doesn't always hold true. Some people act out lies under the influence of alcohol. But not you, Eden. You are true to yourself."

A flush burnt her cheeks. An acute sense of vulnerability made black wells of her eyes. "That night...I'm not sure it can be the same again, Luke."

He stroked her cheek in a tender caress. "Don't worry about it, Eden. I'll make everything right for you," he promised softly. "You don't have to worry about anything."

She gave a nervous little laugh. "Like you did with the Staffords? You'll carefully control my life and responses as you did with them?"

He shook his head. "Not like what I did with them, Eden. Never like that with you." His eyes darkened with what seemed to be deep caring. "What happens between us must be freely given and taken. That's what I mean by our partnership. Understand now?"

She nodded, too choked to speak. He leaned over and brushed her lips with his. It felt like the sealing of a promise. Then he started the car and drove towards the home they would share...until he felt differently about her.

Please let it work, let it last, Eden silently prayed. This seemed more important than anything that had ever happened in her life before. Or would ever happen in the future. As mad as it undoubtedly was, she respected and loved Luke Selby. She desperately wanted to share her whole life with him. Marriage didn't matter.

But children... A painful confusion swirled through Eden's mind. Were children necessary for her happiness? They were a long held dream. But Luke was reality, and right now, being with him was the only thing that mattered. Maybe it was all that mattered.

He turned the car into a modern apartment complex of circular construction built right on the harbour front at Lavender Bay. He operated a remote-control device that opened the door of a private garage. At the end of the garage was a private elevator. They stacked all of Eden's belongings into the small compartment, then rode up to Luke's apartment at the top of the building.

Eden had expected that Luke would not lack any of the material comforts of life, but she could never have anticipated the kind of luxury in which he lived. There was only one word for it—awesome.

The foyer led into a wide curved walkway that formed a sort of mezzanine floor above the sunken living room, which was nothing short of spectacular. Soft leather sofas and armchairs proliferated around glass and chrome tables on which stood fascinating pieces of sculpture. All of them looked out to a curved wall of glass that displayed the Sydney Harbour Bridge in all its night-lit majesty. At the far end of the walkway was the dining area, the modern table and chairs also open to the magnificent view.

There was a central hallway leading off the walkway and Luke turned into it. "We'll put the boxes of books in the study. You can stack them on the shelves at your leisure,'' he said cheerfully.

She followed him to a spacious room that was not only lined with bookshelves, but contained every piece of sophisticated office equipment imaginable. Eden eyed the IBM computer with favour. Maybe Luke would teach her how to use it if she asked him nicely. She had to get some kind of job. She didn't feel right about living off Luke's largesse. Besides, she needed a career for her own survival if she failed to keep his interest.

On their way back to the elevator to collect her other belongings, Luke paused to open another door in the hallway. "Our bedroom," he said, leaning inside to switch on lights. "Have a look around while I get your bags. Dressing room and bathroom are on the far side. You can shove anything of mine out of the way to accommodate your things."

"You might regret saying that," she teased, trying for lightness, although her whole body felt tightly strung at the thought of sharing this with him.

He grinned. "I don't think so, Eden. There's plenty of room to accommodate both of us. And I've observed that you're meticulously tidy."

Eden laughed. "You learn when you're in a home, Luke. Leave anything lying around and it gets stolen."

"This is a different home, Eden," he said softly, his blue eyes warmly caressing her. "Here you can do anything you want."

Her laughter died. "Thank you, Luke," she said huskily.

"My pleasure."

Kind and generous, she reminded herself as she stepped into the bedroom that was about to become theirs. Her heart was thumping like a mighty kettle-drum. Her eyes instantly sought the bed they would share tonight.

It was certainly big enough for both of them. King-size, Eden thought, as was the whole bedroom. It was furnished in blues and greys and white. Very restful. The floor was split-level, the bedroom fittings on the higher level, a private sitting area on the lower level facing another wall of glass. Filmy white curtains blurred the view, but the lights of the city still shone through.

She walked around the bed to the far side where a door obviously led to the rest of the luxurious suite. It opened to a dressing room that contained metres of hanging space, rows of drawers, shoe racks and stacks of shelves. Another door led to a positively decadent bathroom. A huge spa bath was set into the marble floor. The circular shower cubicle was obviously made to hold at least two people. Mirrors seemed to be everywhere. The vanity not only had a marble top, but the cupboards below had gleaming brass doors.

Eden shook her head in wonderment. Was she, Eden Lindsey from Redfern, really going to live in such splendour? Despite all the rich homes she had been housed in since becoming a nanny, never had she seen anything like this. She couldn't help wondering how wealthy Luke was. Certainly this apartment had to be worth... Eden shook her head. The figure was too large.

She took a deep breath. It did nothing to calm her pulse. Luke was raising her to the heights, all right. Eden feverishly hoped the fall would never come. She backed out of the bathroom and returned to the bedroom just as Luke brought in her bags.

He looked at her quizzically. "Something wrong, Eden?"

"No!" she said quickly. "A bit...disoriented. That's all. I just hadn't comprehended that living with you encompassed all this."

"It's simply a place, Eden. A rather empty place when I'm alone," he said quietly. His mouth curled into an ironic little smile. "And I regret that it doesn't have a garden for you."

It brought a smile to her lips. "Well, I'll get my pot-plants tomorrow, anyway."

He nodded towards the wall of curtains. "There's an outside terrace you can fill with flowers if you like. Then we could lie in bed and look out at your garden in the mornings."

The choked-up feeling came back. She heaved a deep sigh to get rid of it. "You're being very good to me, Luke. I hope...I hope I really am what you want."

"Eden, don't be frightened," he said softly, walking towards her. "You have nothing to be frightened of."

"I'm not," she protested. But she was trembling from nervous tension when he drew her into his arms.

"It's all right," he murmured, enfolding her in his warmth and strength. He rubbed his cheek soothingly over her hair. "I'll look after you. You trust me to do that, don't you?"

"Yes," she whispered.

He feathered soft kisses around her temples. Eden shut her eyes tight and concentrated on the feel of his body seeping into hers, the hard power of him that she knew could overwhelm her with exciting sensations. She desperately wanted to close down her mind, forget all the doubts about the future and lose herself in the enthralling magic of Luke's lovemaking.

She wound her arms around his neck and lifted her face to his, her lips quivering in anticipation of the way he would sensitise them with his, then stir all the wild responses he had stirred before.

Yet this time there was no urgent rush to passion. Luke seemed intent on beguiling all her senses with his kissing and touching and the sweet murmured words that kept assuring her she was perfect for him. Controlled, she thought hazily, but her mind didn't want to grasp that concept. It wanted to sift and savour the sensations Luke was weaving through her with consummate artistry.

He took a long time to come to the point. He seemed content to drive her crazy with feeling, drawing her into the intense pleasure of the most intimate secrets. When the moment came, Eden found she was almost dying for him, and her responses were as wild and as fervent as they had been on the night of Marlee's wedding. She didn't need champagne. She didn't need to be intoxicated by anything beyond the beautiful man she was with. The man who made her feel beautiful in everything she was and everything she did. She could be herself because it was Luke she was with.

And all the control he had exerted for her sake slipped away from him as she gave of herself with a totality that knew no inhibitions, a totality that wanted only to please him, to give him all the feelings he gave her, to share this deepest of intimacies with all the intensity of absolute togetherness.

He held her for a long time afterwards, cuddling and stroking her, enjoying the aftermath of ecstatic fulfilment in their embrace of each other. The soft glowing contentment that Eden felt, knowing she had totally satisfied *her* man came from another source of inner satisfaction. As she lay in Luke's arms, tenderly stroking him, the thought came that now she knew what it was like to be a *real* woman. Now she was complete.

It had been the right decision, to come with him, be with him. If it led nowhere further than this, it had still been right. To know what it was to love totally... that was worth knowing whatever the price.

CHAPTER EIGHT

WHILE LUKE was getting ready for work the next morning, Eden set about making space to hang up her clothes in his dressing room. *Their* dressing room, she corrected herself with a satisfied little smile, until she came across the woman-size bathrobe. It was blue, the same as Luke's, but far too small to fit him. Recognising that obvious fact gave Eden a queasy feeling in the pit of her stomach. Had Luke lied to her about his relationships with other women in his life?

She released the suggestive garment in guilty haste as he stepped out of the bathroom, his jaw shiny from shaving and from some expensive male toiletry, which had an attractive tangy smell. His smile for her cut to a slight frown as he noticed the swing of the bathrobe on its hanger. His eyes shot straight to hers, sharply purposeful.

"I'm sorry, Eden. I'd forgotten that was there. I should have removed it before you came," he said apologetically.

"Does it belong to..."

"No-one. A convenience garment," he sliced in quickly. His mouth twisted as he softly stated, "I have had companions who've stayed overnight from time to time. Celibacy does not suit me, Eden. But as I told you before, you are the only woman I've asked to live with me."

Eden couldn't help wondering how many companions there had been. Luke was certainly an expert lover.

"You did have Jeff before me," he reminded her, quietly but ruthlessly setting aside the questions in her eyes. "Now it's us, Eden."

"Yes," she agreed, trying hard to believe Luke felt the same way about her as she felt about him. She had been going to marry Jeff, which was hardly the same thing as a casual affair, but her present arrangement with Luke wasn't casual, either. Not for her.

Was it only satisfying sex for him? What other kind of companionship did he find with her? The uncomplicated kind, she answered herself, the kind that had no pretence. At least, that was what he had told her.

He stepped forward and slid the robe off the hanger.

"You don't have to take it away, Luke," she said decisively.

"I want to." He gave her a rueful smile. "A clean slate, Eden. No shades of anyone else. Only you."

He kissed her then, with a passionate possessiveness that successfully obliterated the thought of any other woman. Yet after he had gone for the day, Eden couldn't help thinking there was no clean slate for her and Luke. The psychological and emotional scars from his brief marriage had written a slate that wasn't about to be wiped clean. Not only that, Eden didn't believe it was natural for anyone not to want children. Something must have turned him against them. But Luke had told her she had to accept him as he was, so there was no point in brooding over what wasn't about to be changed.

As it turned out, the first week with Luke was a taste of paradise to Eden. He indulged her every whim with pleasure dancing in his eyes. Nothing was too much trouble to him, and she delighted in giving him pleasure.

The clothes Luke insisted on buying her from Paula Michaelson were every girl's dream. He banished all concern about flaunting her womanly assets. She was *his* woman. Other men could look to their hearts' content, but anyone who stepped out of line would answer to *him*. It was as if he had thrown a protective ring around her, and it gave Eden a heady feeling of freedom. For the first time in her life, she thoroughly enjoyed being a woman.

He took her to a landscape and garden nursery and insisted she choose whatever she fancied having on the bedroom terrace. Eden had to restrain him from going completely overboard with her favoured selections. After all, they did want to be able to walk out onto the terrace as well as admire the flowers from bed.

He set up discs for her in his computer and helped her with the manuals so that she could master word processing. He discussed the pros and cons of courses she could take that would lead to a number of job opportunities. He encouraged her to make inquiries about all sorts of careers, insisting that she should not put limits on herself. She should select something that would stretch her abilities and give her a sense of challenge and fulfilment.

A cleaning woman, Mrs. Markham, came on Mondays and Thursdays, so there was little housework for Eden to do. However, she took enormous pleasure and pride in surprising Luke with the evening meals she cooked for him. He said they could eat out. He didn't require her to cook for him. But Eden much preferred their private dinners at home together and she had learnt a lot from her close association with cooks in

wealthy households. It delighted her that she could do
something to please Luke, although he certainly seemed
happy just to have her with him.

Eden was deliriously happy. Luke was a wonderful
lover. More than that, he somehow made all the small
intimacies so special—a look, a touch, a smile. He tele-
phoned her from work every day, just to say hello and
ask her what she was doing or thinking, or if there was
anything she'd like him to bring home for her. She could
not imagine a more considerate or caring man.

Occasionally it flitted across her mind that this was a
honeymoon period. She couldn't expect it to last. No
two people lived together in absolute harmony for very
long. When the novelty of having got what he wanted
wore off for Luke... But she didn't want to think about
that. There was no point in crossing bridges until she
came to them.

However, as their first week together came to an end,
Eden was all too aware that there was another honeymoon that was almost over. Marlee and Ray would be
back on Saturday, and neither of them was aware of
what had happened between her and Luke. Eden suspected that Pam Harcourt would have heard by now
through Paula Michaelson, but Luke had made no
mention of his sister, and Eden was reluctant to bring
the subject up.

Nevertheless, Marlee had to be told or she would be
ringing up the Stafford household the moment she and
Ray were settled into Ray's apartment. Eden agonised
over how to break the news to her friend because Marlee was expecting to come home and find Eden en-
gaged to Jeff Southgate. In the end, she wrote her a
brief note, telling her she had left her employment with
the Staffords and she could be contacted at this new

telephone number. Which was the number at Luke's apartment. But she didn't tell Marlee that. Explanations were better face to face, Eden decided.

Marlee's call came on Saturday morning.

Luke was taking a shower so it was Eden who answered the telephone. From the moment she heard Marlee's voice it was obvious that someone had already broken the news to her.

"Eden?" A thread of uncertainty, disbelief.

Eden's heart sank, but she pushed a cheerful note into her voice. "Hi, Marlee! Welcome home! How was the honeymoon?"

A pause. "Eden, are you really living with Luke?" Complete bewilderment.

Eden sighed. "I'm sorry if I've shocked you, Marlee. I wanted to tell you first. Since you left, things...just happened to me."

"Are you happy?"

"I feel wonderful. Complete. I'm sorry, Marlee, but I do."

Another pause. "I don't understand, Eden. What happened to Jeff? You were in love with him."

It was the closest Marlee would ever get to an accusation of being unfaithful, Eden thought ruefully. She tried to find the right words.

"You remember the call I got on the morning of the wedding? That was Jeff to say he'd found someone else and he was never coming back to me."

"Oh, Eden!" Distress poured from her voice.

"So that was finished, there and then," Eden put in matter-of-factly, hoping to dismiss any sense of trauma.

"How could he do it to you?" Marlee cried, sounding even more upset.

"He did!" Eden clipped out.

"And you pretended all day... Oh, Eden! That must have been so terrible!"

"Marlee, your wedding was so beautiful..."

"You had to *pretend* to be happy! For my sake!"

"I was happy for you... and Luke helped an awful lot. I didn't have to pretend, Marlee. I didn't think about it. That was all."

"Oh, Eden!" A shuddering breath. "Why did Jeff call it off? Why—"

"Better career prospects," Eden cut in with more harshness than she had intended. She lightened her voice to careless flippancy. "He got the boss's daughter."

Marlee muttered something fierce that Eden couldn't quite catch. Then she took a deep breath. "So now you're with Luke," she stated flatly, finally accepting it but obviously not liking it.

"Luke is very good to me, Marlee," Eden said gently. "I've never been happier in my life. I'll explain it all to you when I see you. Please don't worry about me. I'm fine. I hope you're as happy as I am."

A pause for consideration. "Yes. Yes, I am. Except about you. I never thought that you..."

Eden took a deep breath. "I did. I guess... I guess Luke changed my mind for me, Marlee. But everything's fine. You'll see when we're together."

"If you say so," came the doubting reply.

"Have you got the photographs from the wedding yet?" Eden asked brightly, changing the subject.

"Yes. Pam picked them up for me. Ray and I are going over there for lunch tomorrow to look through all of them with the family. I wanted you to come, too. Do you think..."

A long hesitation.

"What?" Eden prompted. "You know you can say anything to me, Marlee."

A sigh. "Well, Pam didn't know if you and Luke would come. She's in a bit of a tizzy about what has happened between you two. She thinks she might have offended you. And Luke was very short with her the day after the wedding. So she thinks she's offended him, too. But I want you to come, Eden. And Pam says it's fine with her if it's all right with you."

Tears pricked Eden's eyes. Marlee was loyal to the bone. She would stand by her even if she never understood why Eden was apparently acting so out of character.

"Thank you, Marlee," she said huskily. "I'll have to ask Luke. If it doesn't work out, perhaps we could meet on Monday for lunch. If that's convenient for you."

Marlee quickly agreed, concern still threading her voice, and the call ended on that uncertain note.

Strange how life changes, Eden thought sadly. It would never have happened before. Both she and Marlee had to consider their partners before making any commitment. Of course, there would be less awkwardness if she and Luke were married. But that was never going to happen so it was no use brooding about it.

Luke's instincts seemed to be finely tuned where Eden was concerned. He came out of the bathroom, took one look at her and asked, "What's wrong, Eden?"

She explained about Marlee's call and the secondhand invitation to lunch with his sister's family.

Luke took control. "I'll fix that," he said. A call to his sister was all that was needed. He informed Eden they were warmly welcomed to Sunday lunch.

Eden looked at him questioningly. "Marlee said you were short with Pam the day after the wedding."

He shrugged. "I simply set her straight on a few matters."

"About me?" Eden asked curiously.

"About you and me and life in general." He grinned. "You have nothing to worry about, Eden."

Not while Luke was at her side, Eden thought wryly. He was a slayer of dragons par excellence! And yet... She wondered how *he* would justify the situation to Marlee. He wouldn't, Eden decided. Having got what he wanted, Luke needed no justification, either for himself or for anyone else. He would explain himself to no-one.

However, life wasn't quite so simple, Eden reflected the next day. She was certainly at Luke's side. And dressed in the Paula Michaelson clothes that proclaimed her a fitting partner for him. Her jeans and T-shirt were things of the past. She wore designer-original flared slacks and a matching top in a vibrant violet with lime-green accents. Luke had declared she looked stunning in them. Her outfit stunned Pam and Marlee, too. But only momentarily.

There was no trouble with the Harcourts. Pam and her husband had apparently decided, possibly at Luke's forceful direction, to treat Eden and Luke as an established couple. Not for one moment did their manner deviate from this concept.

Pam was gracious and friendly towards Eden. It was as though that scene after the wedding day had never happened. She accepted Eden as if she had been living with Luke for years, even making a point of saying how well suited they both looked in the wedding photographs. She brought several of them to their particular attention. The twins, of course, saw nothing the least bit untoward about any of the adults' behaviour.

Despite this family acceptance, it was all too apparent to Eden that no amount of glossing over was going to convince Marlee all was well. Not even Luke's gesture of ordering a complete set of the wedding photographs for Eden had any mollifying effect on the fact that Marlee was patently disturbed by this new development.

Nor did Ray seem content to accept the status quo. His wife was upset by it. Ray was concerned. He accepted Marlee's point of view. Several times Eden saw him look wonderingly at his older brother. Luke, she noted, was totally unperturbed. He had his own values and he was not going to live to anybody else's.

Lunch was an al fresco affair of salads and barbecued steak on the patio at poolside. It eventually finished with a casual serving of summer fruits and cheeses. Marlee pressed Pam to stay seated while she and Eden carried the used plates into the kitchen to stack them in the dishwasher.

"Luke isn't right for you," she said as soon as they were out of earshot of the others. Her lovely amber eyes were both urgent and anxious.

"I think he is, Marlee," Eden answered quietly, then gave her a reassuring smile. "You said yourself how kind and generous he is. And he's a lot more than that, besides."

"But he won't marry you," Marlee argued. "Pam says there's no hope of that. He was soured off marriage by what happened with his first wife, and it twisted him up inside."

"What did happen?" Eden asked curiously.

Marlee shook her head. "Luke won't talk about it. All Pam knows is that his ex-wife was pregnant at the time they married. They parted soon after the baby was born. But whatever happened, it was bad enough to turn Luke very hard and cynical where women are concerned.''

Her soft voice gathered more concern as she added, ''And it turned him off children, as well, Eden. He never goes to see his own child. He never visited here when the twins were babies. Even now he keeps his distance from them, although he treats them nicely when they demand his attention. I hadn't really noticed until Pam mentioned it, but it's true. Luke doesn't like children. He mostly avoids having anything to do with them. Look at him. He's doing it now.''

Eden glanced at the family group. Pam and her husband and Ray were laughing over something with the twins. Luke sat apart from them, his face a hard, expressionless mask, his gaze directed at some sparrows pecking grains from a bird feeder that hung on one of the trees.

Eden heaved a sigh, stifling a little stab of pain. She fiercely told herself that Luke was all she wanted, then turned to Marlee. Her friend rushed straight into more speech, her eyes pleading with Eden.

''I know how hurt you must have been when Jeff let you down like that. But Luke isn't the answer. You know that's true. No matter how good he is to you at the moment. And I hate to say this, but you always swore you'd never be used by a man, Eden. You know you did. And Luke...''

''Perhaps I'm using him, Marlee,'' she put in lightly. *I'm not lonely any more,* she told herself. *Luke is good for me. We're good together!*

Shock hit her friend's face and then was summarily dismissed. ''No! I don't believe that, Eden. And you can't make me believe it. It's because of Jeff. You took

Luke on the rebound. It was because I wasn't here. Luke was."

Eden gave a defensive little laugh. "Do you really think I'm that weak, Marlee?" Her black eyes tried to reassure her friend. "I know Luke won't marry me. He told me so. He's very honest. He doesn't want children. He's honest about that, too. He even told me he was being totally unfair. I also know what I'm facing. I know what we have together probably won't last. But, Marlee, I want Luke. I need him. And I love him. And while he wants me, and I'm good for him, I'll stay with him."

Marlee searched her face with deep concern. "You love him, Eden? You can love a man like that?"

"Yes," she replied simply. "I'm sorry if you feel I'm . . . letting us both down."

Tears suddenly welled into the soft amber eyes. "Oh, Eden! You've meant so much to me all these years. And I'm so perfectly happy. . . and you're going to be made so miserable. You'll never have. . . you'll never have your dreams fulfilled."

The dreams were there, shimmering between them. All they had talked about in the dark nights of their growing-up years together. The dreams that had sustained them through the time when they had so little control over anything that happened to them, when their lives were not really their own. When choices were few and so much that they hated was forced upon them.

Eden felt her heart breaking into little pieces. The dreams they had shared were beautiful, perfect, complete. She didn't want to face up to them, or confront the splintered shards of those dreams. She had to be strong.

"There are other dreams, Marlee." She didn't know if that was true, but she had to cling to some belief in the face of what she felt with Luke.

"Yes," Marlee said quickly, blinking back the tears. "I want you to be happy. If you're happy..."

"I am." Eden forced her lips into an appealing smile. "I truly am."

Marlee nodded. Several times. "You've always got me to turn to, Eden."

"I know."

"Any time," Marlee insisted fiercely. "Whatever happens."

Eden was deeply touched. "I know that, Marlee. Thank you."

The luncheon party broke up soon afterwards. Luke was unusually self-contained on the drive from St. Ives to Lavender Bay. He offered no conversation. Eden had the forceful impression that he was brooding over something. She tried to draw him out with a couple of comments about the wedding photographs, but his brief replies were not encouraging. She lapsed into silence, wondering if she had done something wrong.

Once they were in his apartment, Eden brightly offered to brew some coffee for them, hoping Luke would shrug off whatever was on his mind. He trailed along to the kitchen after her, and leaned against one of the benches while she ground the coffee beans and set the percolator going. She was extremely conscious of him watching her. Finally she couldn't bear it any longer. She swung around and confronted him.

"What's the matter, Luke?"

He didn't deny that something was wrong. There was a closed, guarded look on his face. Although his pose against the cupboards was apparently relaxed, there was enough tension emanating from him to play havoc with Eden's nerves.

"Ray insisted on taking me aside for a man-to-man talk this afternoon," he stated flatly.

"Well?" Eden prompted.

"Well, what?" he retorted, poker-faced.

Eden heaved a sigh. "I guess Marlee put him up to it. She is a very loving and gentle person. She gave me a woman-to-woman talk. She doesn't think you're right for me. I have set her straight on that point, Luke."

The blue eyes probed hers intently. "I guess I want you to set me straight on a few points, Eden," he said quietly.

"Like what?" she asked in puzzlement.

"I asked you at the wedding if it was serious with Jeff Southgate. Your reply was, *not very*."

Eden frowned. There was an intonation of wounded pride in Luke's voice. "So?" she asked, still not sure what he was getting at. "I can hardly be very serious with a man who doesn't want me any more. I did tell you later on that Jeff had called it off. What more do you want me to say?"

"You didn't tell me he had virtually jilted you at the altar, Eden," he said softly. "Nor that the marriage had been planned for three months' time, and you were expecting Jeff to buy you an engagement ring that week. Nor how very much in love with him you'd been. Furthermore, you were never so specific as to say that all these events had taken place on the very morning of the wedding."

Eden could feel herself flushing over how much of a fool she had been with Jeff. She knew now that she had been more in love with the idea of love and marriage than with the man himself.

Luke watched the warm colour suffuse her cheeks, his eyes burning with a brightness that looked like intense emotion to Eden. "I was under the impression that you'd had an affair that had fallen short of becoming very serious," he said. "But that wasn't the case, was it?"

"When Jeff called me the morning of the wedding, I felt it was the end of the world. But life goes on, Luke. And I learnt it wasn't the end of the world."

That truth didn't seem to mollify him. "Ray suggested to me this afternoon that you were not in an emotionally stable state," he said, his eyes intently watchful for any reaction from her. "He further suggested that your decision to come and live with me was a rebound response. And that it was unbecoming of me to take advantage of a woman in deep emotional trauma."

"Do you care?" Eden asked, angry that he was questioning her motives.

His face tightened. "Yes. I care," he bit out.

"But you got what you wanted, Luke," she reminded him.

"I don't care to be a substitute lover for anyone," he sliced at her, an edge of bitterness sharpening his voice.

She saw the hard pride stamped on his face, the need to be wanted for himself written in his eyes, and knew that Ray's words to him had raised uncertainties that Luke didn't want to live with.

"I want *you*, Luke," she said softly. "I don't know how you did it, but you wiped Jeff out of my life the night of the wedding. Is that what you need to hear?"

"If it's the truth," he said curtly, the blue eyes boring into hers.

She walked over to him and slowly slid her hands up his chest, her eyes openly shining her love for him...if he had the perception to see it. "Do you think I would have been so happy with you this past week if you weren't the man I wanted, Luke? Do you really believe I could pretend all that?"

She saw the relief and renewed certainty pour into his eyes, soften his face. "Eden..." It was a sigh of pent-up desire.

Her hands slid up around his neck as she pressed herself closer to the taut strength of his body. "I want you, Luke. You, now, here. Please?"

His arms came round her, scooping her hard against him, his hands running feverishly over her body, moulding her desire to his. His mouth hungered over hers, invaded it with a passion that had no semblance of any control whatsoever. Although it wasn't the most comfortable place to make love—there and then against the kitchen cupboards—somehow it meant more to Eden than all the lovemaking there had been between them. She wrapped her legs around him with the sweetest sense of possession and exulted in the wildness of his desire for her.

Luke might not love her as she loved him, but he certainly didn't like the thought of her not being satisfied with what they had together. Eden discounted any thought that it was a matter of pride or self-esteem. She knew intuitively it was a deep basic need crying out to be met—a need for truly committed sharing that he could trust implicitly—the need to be not alone.

She vaguely heard the percolator bubbling madly. It clicked itself off. The frenzied tempest of Luke's desire reached its peak and subsided.

He carried Eden into the bedroom with him and lowered her onto the pillows. He slowly dispensed with her remaining clothes, kissing her all over in a slow, sensual worshipping that sent shivers of pleasure rippling over her skin. It was as though he wanted her to know she was precious to him and he was telling her so with every touch of his lips and hands.

Eden wanted to say she loved him, that it was all right, that he was safe with her, but she wasn't sure it was what he wanted. Luke might think she was pressing him to say he loved her. He had never spoken of love, only simply of sharing their lives together.

So be it, Eden thought. It was enough. But she couldn't help silently cursing the woman who had turned him off marriage and children. Who had turned him off trusting other women, trusting in promises. She wished he would tell her about it. She wished she could ask. But she knew she never would.

"You have to take me as I am," he had said. And that was what she had to do. So she gently paused to help him off with the rest of his clothes, and she kissed and touched him to let him know how precious he was to her. All the more precious because she had only him to replace the other dreams, which could never come true.

CHAPTER NINE

WITH ALL DOUBTS about their pleasure in each other erased, Eden was sublimely happy with Luke. She decided to let the idea of getting a job slide for a while. After all, it had been ten months since her last holiday from work, and she deserved some time off to relax and simply be there for Luke.

On Tuesday morning Paula Michaelson called to ask if Eden could come in for a fitting. "You'll want this evening dress for Thursday night," she pressed, "so if you can make time today, we can get it finished."

Eden agreed on eleven o'clock as suitable, then rang Luke to ask what was supposed to be happening on Thursday night that she needed an evening dress for.

He chuckled. "I completely forgot. See what a distraction you've become to me? It's just as well Paula is on the ball."

"So where are we going?" Eden pressed.

"I have season tickets to the opera premieres. *The Merry Widow* opens on Thursday. We'll be meeting up with a number of people—including the Staffords—and after the show, we'll be having supper in the Benelong Restaurant at the Opera House. Now don't start worrying about it. I promise you that both Paula and I will see that you're the star of the night," he added teasingly.

She laughed. "If you say so."

"I do. And I know you'll love *The Merry Widow,* so it should be a grand night out. Remind me to play it for you when I get home. I've got a recording of it on disc somewhere."

"Okay. I'll look forward to it."

Eden felt like a princess on Thursday night. Paula had designed a fantastic gown in lipstick-pink taffeta. It was strapless and narrow-skirted and showed off every curve of Eden's figure to svelte advantage. Little tucks in two lighter pinks made a special feature of the bustline and hipline, and a rose fashioned in three shades of pink was attached to a ribbon tied around Eden's neck so that the rose rested below one ear. Remembering how Luke had liked her hair in curls, Eden had splashed out on going to a hairdresser to have her hair especially styled for the evening, and the cascade of curls was swept to one side so that the rose could be properly featured.

Her reward was the pride and pleasure that shone from Luke's eyes. He looked every bit the handsome prince in evening dress, Eden thought happily, and her night at the opera was indeed a marvellous night to remember.

The production was absolutely magical. The supper afterwards in the Benelong Restaurant was all elegant luxury. Luke's friends readily accepted her as one of them. Paula's design was extravagantly admired by the women with some envy, by the men with pleasure in the way Eden displayed it. Champagne flowed. Luke's eyes said there was not a woman in the world to match her. Eden bubbled with joy.

It was not until the following week that the first niggle of worry dimmed her happiness. What should have been happening wasn't. Not that she had ever been absolutely to-the-day regular, Eden reminded herself. There were times in the past that she had gone six or seven weeks between periods. Although it had been a few years since that had occurred, it didn't mean it couldn't happen again. A few days over...it meant nothing. It couldn't mean anything. It was unthinkable now that she was with Luke. She put it out of her mind. She was late. That was all.

Eden successfully ignored the niggle of worry for another wonderful week, but the days kept adding up. Her breasts started to feel very sensitive. She told herself it was because of the way Luke caressed them when they made love. She told herself that her hormones were probably out of kilter from all the physical excitement she was experiencing with Luke. She told herself that what she feared couldn't possibly have happened. Not from the only mad, reckless night of her life. And she had taken precautions since then.

Paula Michaelson's designs for her were being completed and delivered. She had to wear them for Luke. He had paid for them. So much money, to please her and reassure her in her partnership with him. It would be criminal if they were to be wasted. She simply couldn't be pregnant from that one night. Fate wouldn't deal her such a low blow. Not after all she had been through in her childhood. Not when it would mean losing the man she loved.

No. Her body was simply playing tricks on her. That was all.

Another week went by. Eden got up one morning to go to the bathroom and was instantly hit by dizziness and a sudden surge of nausea. She just made it to the bowl before her stomach convulsively heaved its contents. She leaned there, shuddering in reaction. A cold sweat broke out on her forehead. It couldn't be, it couldn't be, her mind keep reciting in forlorn, desperate protest. How long she stayed there in limp helplessness she didn't know. There was a knock on the bathroom door.

"Eden, are you all right?"

Luke calling. Luke, who didn't want children. *Especially not children*. Oh, God! How could you do this to me? Eden silently wailed in despair. Haven't I been through enough misery? Haven't I tried and tried to be a decent human being? Why this? Why, when I've finally found someone who makes my life worth living? What have I fought for all these years? To lose all that means so much to me now?

"Eden?"

"Yes. I'm fine, Luke," she lied. I've never lied to him before, she thought wretchedly. All her survival instincts rushed to her aid, helping her to pull herself together. She opened the door and gave him a rueful smile. "I must be getting my period. That's all. I've got a rather long cycle and it always hits me hard," she lied again, desperately protecting what she had with him.

He made a sympathetic grimace. "I guess it had to come sooner or later." Then with more concern, "You don't look at all well, Eden. Go back to bed and I'll bring you some coffee."

He was kind and nice to her. Eden felt the most dreadful fraud. But how could she tell him the truth? And it might not be true. She hadn't taken a pregnancy test. Maybe she would get her period today. Or tomorrow. Maybe that was why she felt sick. Maybe there was simply something wrong with her. She would go and see a doctor after Luke had left for work. A doctor might give her some other explanation, not pregnancy. Please, please, she prayed. Not pregnancy.

Luke went to work.

Eden went to see a doctor.

She was pregnant. About seven weeks, the doctor said. He said a lot of other things about caring for herself but they floated over Eden's head. It isn't fair, she kept thinking. It just isn't fair.

But it was a fact of life that she had to face. Along with the fact that Luke didn't want a child, didn't want anything to do with children. The moment she told him an awful chill of rejection would ice his eyes. She knew it would. And that would be the end of the relationship she had shared with him. Everything would change.

He wouldn't want her around him any more. He might keep her out of a sense of responsibility, but they would both end up hating that. He would probably offer to settle her somewhere, even pay child support, but he wouldn't come and visit. He didn't visit the child he already had. He would buy another blue bathrobe and have companions who weren't loaded down with a child. That was what he would do.

Eden shuddered. She didn't want to face up to that bleak future. Not yet. It wasn't fair. As the day wore on, she was gripped more and more by a feverish need to keep the status quo with Luke, to postpone the shattering moment of truth, to cling to the happiness she had known with him.

Why not have as much time as she could with him? she argued to herself. Pack a lifetime of loving into the few short months left before her pregnancy started showing. If she dieted, exercised, held back the inevitable end as long as she could, would that be so wrong?

Luke wanted her with him. She wanted to be with him. If she had to tell him a few little untruths to preserve what small amount of happiness they could have together, wasn't that forgivable in the circumstances? After all, Luke deserved value for all the money he had spent on her, and it couldn't be too wrong of her to give him what she could while she could. Only when the child in her womb could not be hidden any longer would she tell him the truth.

When the end came, as it must, she would leave without asking anything of him. She couldn't bear to be a financial parasite on him for the rest of his life. Not when he had made it so clear that he didn't want a child. She would find a place for herself, get a job where her employers would be accommodating about her condition…if such a job could be found. Failing that, she did have money in the bank, enough to see her through the birth of her baby…Luke's baby. At least she would always have a part of him to love.

If the worse came to the worst, she could apply for the unmarried mother's pension. She would survive. It might mean being reduced to the same slum living conditions that she had known in her childhood, but she *would* survive. And she would build her life again. She had to, for the child's sake. Her child. Luke's child.

For the next four nights Luke simply held her cuddled warmly against him in bed. Eden hated the deception she was playing on him, but she kept telling herself it was justified, and she couldn't help loving his tender consideration of her. In the mornings she stayed in bed, sucking a glucose lolly while Luke used the bathroom first. It helped to settle the nausea when she got up. On the fifth night she inititiated the lovemaking Luke quickly responded to, happy to resume the intimacy he had not pressed while she was supposedly indisposed.

Life with Luke went on as before. Eden made inquiries about a course entitled General Business Purposes that encompassed clerical applications on computer, word processing and filing systems. The course had already been running two weeks but Eden didn't have time to wait for the next course to start. She figured she could catch up the work if she really applied herself. After all, she wouldn't be starting off totally ignorant about computers.

Luke was happy to go along with this decision. He seemed happy to go along with anything Eden decided. However, what with working hard at the course and leading a busy social life with Luke, Eden found herself getting extremely tired. She took the iron tablets the doctor had prescribed, but they didn't seem to help much. She had long afternoon naps at weekends, deliberately provoking Luke into making love with her, which he never tired of doing, so he would think it was fairly natural for her to fall asleep afterwards.

The precious time with him slipped by all too quickly. Eden panicked when she realised her waist was thickening and there was nothing she could do about it. Diet and exercise didn't help. Fortunately Luke didn't seem to notice. The problem was with the clothes that Paula Michaelson had designed and made for her. Some of them became impossible to wear. Eden made little adjustments to those that lent themselves to adjustments. She coped as best she could, but she knew time was running out on her. Moving a button here, letting out a seam there were only stop-gap measures.

She couldn't—literally couldn't—bring herself to pretend to have another period. She was greedy for everything she shared with Luke. So little time. So much to store in her memory. She had to get the maximum out of every minute with him. Besides which, she had told him she had a long cycle. He wouldn't be counting the weeks that passed.

If there was a slightly brittle edge to her brilliant gaiety in his company, a quality of desperation in her lovemaking, a reluctance to let him out of her sight, Luke didn't seem to notice. He appeared to be absolutely content with their living together.

Eden rigidly kept her inner despair hidden from everyone, even Marlee. They usually met for lunch once a week, and Eden invariably put on a happy face for her friend. She didn't know how she was going to cope when the time of revelation came, and she continued to stave it off to the very last moment.

But not even the grimmest determination was proof against some circumstances. At one of their lunches, Marlee glowingly told Eden that she was pregnant. All the right words formed up in Eden's mind, but she couldn't make her mouth work. Tears welled into her eyes and overflowed. She tried to stop them. She had no right to mar her friend's happiness. It was just that she ached to be happy about having her baby, too.

The glow on Marlee's face faded into deep distress. She reached across the little cafe table where they were seated and squeezed Eden's hand. "I'm sorry, Eden. I guess it reminded you that..." She bit her lip and looked agonised.

"I'm pregnant, too," Eden blurted out.

Then somehow she couldn't hold any of her private anguish in any longer. And Marlee kept holding her hand, squeezing it gently, lovingly, sympathetically, and the roles of their adolescence were strangely reversed, with Marlee being the strong one and Eden leaning on her friend's strength.

"I have to leave him soon," she finally choked out.

"Eden, Luke seems very happy with you. Don't you think there's a chance that..."

"No. I couldn't bear it, Marlee, knowing he doesn't really want the child. Keeping me on sufferance because... because I was stupid."

"He's responsible as well as you."

"No." Eden shook her head vehemently. "It was all my fault. It has to be a clean break. There's no other way."

"Then come and stay with Ray and me," Marlee offered impulsively.

"No. I couldn't." No way in the world would she be an interfering third party to Marlee's marriage, a wet blanket on Ray's and Marlee's happiness. "I'll start looking for a place next week. I'll find something. Please don't worry about that. I've got enough money to keep myself for a while. If I can get a job—" she shook her head miserably "—if someone will employ me..."

Marlee frowned over the problem. "I think Ray could give you a job in his office if you'd like that, Eden. One of the girls there is going on maternity leave next month. You could take her place. Get experience. It would only be temporary but... Would you like me to ask him about it?"

"Yes... No... Oh, I don't know, Marlee. With Ray being Luke's brother..."

"Please—" the soft amber eyes begged compliance "—let me help you this much, Eden. It's not as if Ray's office has anything to do with Luke. He needn't know. If I ask Ray not to tell him, he won't. I promise you."

Eden gulped down the lump in her throat. "I've made a mess of this, haven't I? And I'm really glad for you, Marlee. Starting the family you dreamed about."

"I know, Eden. And I've always wanted the best for you, too. You've looked after me so much. Now I want to help you. I'll feel a lot better if you'll consider the job with Ray," she pressed anxiously.

"If you're sure it would be available," Eden conceded gratefully. It would be one load off her mind even though she felt it was probably a coward's way out of her dilemma.

Marlee smiled her relief. "I'll ring you tomorrow."

"Thanks, Marlee. I'm sorry I—"

"Don't, Eden," Marlee said vehemently. "I'm glad you told me. You should have told me before. Aren't I your friend that you tell everything to?"

Eden managed a shaky smile. "Well, I've certainly loaded it on you today, my friend."

"That's what friends are for," Marlee stated firmly. "And if you want help in looking for a place you must ring me, Eden. Promise?"

"I promise."

Marlee rang the next day to say the job was Eden's, starting in a month's time if that suited her. Eden replied that it did, and asked Marlee to pass on her gratitude to Ray.

Eden didn't tell Luke that Ray and Marlee were going to have a baby. She couldn't trust herself not to get emotional about it and she didn't want to see Luke's indifference to the news.

Another weekend came. Eden and Luke were invited to a dinner party. For some reason Luke took it into his head to look through Eden's wardrobe of designer clothes and choose the dress he wanted her to wear to the party. To Eden's intense relief it was styled to skim her figure to her hips, where it flared into swinging gores. It was also black, which was slimming. She was fast losing any pretensions to a waist, but at least she wasn't bulging yet.

She was dressed and ready to go when Luke insisted she stand still and close her eyes. She felt him place something around her neck and her heart sank. In all conscience she couldn't accept anything more from him. Only one more week, maybe two, and she had to walk out of his life forever. Luke had already made a teasing comment about her putting on weight. Not that he minded. He had laughingly said that Rubens's well-fleshed women always appealed to him.

It was a long rope of pearls. Real pearls, which must have cost him a small fortune.

He grinned at her. "I had a friend buy them for you in Japan. Like them?"

Eden could feel the blood draining from her face. She couldn't tell him to take them back to whatever shop he'd bought them from. "They're . . . they're beautiful, Luke," she choked out. "But I don't want you buying jewellery for me. I can't accept it," she said in quiet desperation and started to lift the precious rope over her head.

"Why not?" Luke argued, stopping her action. He frowned at her. "I want you to have them, Eden. I got them especially for you."

Pearls are for tears, she thought. "I don't feel comfortable about it, Luke," she pleaded. "So much money . . ."

He shrugged. "Surely I can spend my money how I please." The blue eyes twinkled a totally shameless appeal. "And it pleases me to see you wearing them. So leave them on, Eden. For me."

He made it so hard. "All right," she conceded reluctantly. "But they're your pearls, Luke. Not mine. Please remember that."

Again he frowned, then dismissed her protest. "They're yours and you can wear them whenever you like."

The rope around her neck felt as though it was choking her all night. More than ever before it felt wrong to go on pretending. She had to end it. Yet the thought of losing Luke forever was sheer agony for her.

What had to be done, had to be done, she told herself sternly.

Once the weekend was over she started looking for a place to live. The rentals for even modest bed-sitters were frightening. She finally found something she felt she could afford in Glebe. It was a cheaply furnished bed-sitting room with an adjoining bathroom. She had to share a kitchen with three other people but she thought she could cope with that. The private bathroom was the important thing.

She signed a lease, paid over the bond and a month's rental in advance, shivered at the thought that Glebe was uncomfortably close to Redfern, then told herself that it was better for her to be situated on the other side of the harbour to Luke, and that at least there was bus transportation virtually from her door to Ray's city office.

Having settled on her bolthole, there was nothing stopping her from taking her leave of Luke, except the terrible pain in her heart. One last night, she promised herself, one long night of loving that would have to be her final memory.

She cooked Luke's favourite things for dinner. She put a bottle of champagne on ice. She stacked a number of compact discs for playing, the ones she and Luke especially liked. She set the dining room table with candles and flowers. She put on a silk lounging suit, which was a brilliant swirl of blues.

"Are we having company?" Luke asked when he came home and saw the romantic setting on the table.

"No. Just us," Eden said, sliding her arms around his neck.

He cocked an inquiring eyebrow at her. "Have I missed something special? Your birthday?"

She laughed and shook her head. Then her black eyes glowed all her love at him. "Every night has been special with you, Luke. Every night and every day. I want you to know that."

"For me, too," he said softly, and kissed her lovingly.

It was a beautiful night, everything Eden had wanted it to be and more. Eventually she fell asleep in Luke's arms, and when she woke to his touch in the morning, it was to find him already up and dressed for work.

"I brought you coffee," he said with a nod at the steaming mug on her bedside table. Then he leaned down and dropped a kiss on her forehead. "I'm late already, so I've got to run."

There was no time to reach her arms up and hold him for a moment longer. He moved away even as he spoke. Eden watched him stride briskly to the bedroom door. He waved at her and said, "Goodbye." Then he was gone.

With a heavy, grieving heart, Eden packed all her old things, none of the new that Luke had bought for her. She hired a taxi to transport all her belongings across the city to her new address. The rented room couldn't take all her pot-plants, so she selected only four and left the rest. It was a long, draining day, and she was pale with exhaustion when she returned to Luke's apartment for the final goodbye.

She spent the last of the waiting time out on the garden terrace. She imagined Luke would get rid of all the plants after she had gone. He wouldn't want any reminder of her.

When he was due home, she went to the kitchen, placed her handbag and the card for a taxi beside the telephone, then leaned against the counter, trying to order her thoughts into what she had to say.

CHAPTER TEN

"EDEN?" Luke's voice rang with happy anticipation.

Eden swallowed hard and called out to him. "I'm in the kitchen, Luke."

This was the dreaded moment. She heard the soft footfalls along the walkway. They sounded like death knells to her. Her heart beat with slow, heavy thuds. Beads of perspiration broke out on her forehead. The palms of her hands felt hot and damp.

Luke reached the kitchen doorway, a smile lighting his darkly handsome face, blue eyes dancing their pleasure at being home...with her. He raised his eyebrows in teasing inquiry. "Nothing cooking tonight?"

Her lips moved stiffly to form the word No, and her voice cooperated in a croaky fashion.

He frowned as he saw her wipe her hands down the side of the floppy T-shirt. The frown deepened as he took in her old stretch jeans. His gaze skated to her face, eyes sharp now, taking in the clammy paleness of her skin, the feverish brilliance of her black eyes.

"Are you sick, Eden?" he asked in quick concern.

Yes, she thought. Sick at heart, sick in mind, sick to her very soul. Yet she nursed a fragile little hope that Luke really loved her, and he might revise his feeling about not having a child...their child. There was a chance, wasn't there?

No risks, no prizes.

She took a deep breath and prayed fiercely for a prize. "I'm pregnant, Luke."

The words spilled out weakly but they hit him with devastating effect. The blue eyes glazed with shock. She saw the colour drain from his face, leaving it a bleak landscape of hard planes and angles. His mouth thinned into a grim line. His chest rose and fell as though his lungs had been punched. His hands clenched at his sides.

There was a terrible stillness about him, the kind of stillness that somehow screamed of nerves stretched to breaking point and inner turbulence about to erupt. Eden's chest felt unbearably tight, and she belatedly realised she was holding her breath. There was a ringing in her ears. Her pulse was pounding at her temples. She forced herself to breathe again. Waiting for Luke to speak was excruciating.

"What do you want to do about it?" he asked in a flat toneless voice.

Eden stared at him, noting the total lack of expression on his face. It was stony. Giving nothing away. Waiting to pass judgement, she thought. Her fragile little hope withered and died. What are *you* going to do. Not *we*. It was her pregnancy. Nothing to do with him. She dully wondered if he wanted her to say she would have an abortion. Her hand instinctively lifted and spread protectively over the slight mound of her stomach.

"I'm going to have the baby," she said.

Another silence, thick with tension. She saw Luke uncurl his hands then clench them again. His mouth slowly twisted into a sardonic grimace. A savage mockery glittered into the blue eyes.

"So that was what last night was about," he said softly. "Sweetening the pill before you delivered it."

That hurt. It hurt so badly she couldn't speak. She stared dumbly at him, her gaze running distractedly over his strongly muscled shoulders, his broad chest, the long powerful legs that had been entwined with hers last night. Didn't he know it had been an act of love? Didn't he sense how desperately she needed him to take her in his arms right now and tell her it was all right? Couldn't he see her agony?

"Why, Eden?" he asked, not making one move towards her. "Wasn't living together enough for you? Did you have to try pressuring for marriage and children? Did you think you could *persuade* me into it?"

The quiet words carried an intense bitterness. She realised he was probably thinking of the marriage he had gone through with before because the woman was pregnant, but that didn't alleviate the pain she felt. He had no right to make such assumptions about *her.* She had accepted his terms. If she had known... Well, it was far too late to blame herself for not checking first. She shook her head. Impossible to put spilled milk back in the bottle.

"It just happened, Luke," she forced out through dry lips. "I didn't plan it."

He gave a harsh derisive laugh. "I gave you fair warning that I didn't want children. Pregnancy doesn't *just happen* these days, Eden. "

"I'm sorry," she said miserably. "More sorry than you'll ever know, Luke. But I can't help that now. It's done, and there's no undoing it."

No response from him. The blue eyes bored into her without mercy, without love. Eden stifled her anguish and lifted her chin in a show of independent pride. Her black eyes fiercely challenged his derision.

"I was saying goodbye to you last night, Luke. That was what it was about. I thought it wasn't right to walk out of your life without any explanation. It is your child as well as mine, and although I'm well aware that you don't want it, I thought you should know about it. So I came back to tell you."

"Came back?" His brow lowered in puzzlement.

"Yes. I've moved all my things to a place of my own. I don't deny you gave me fair warning. So under the circumstances, I thought a clean break was best. I'm not asking you to look after me, Luke."

"Of course I'll look after you!" he shot back at her angrily. "What kind of man do you think I am?"

She ignored his words, rushing on with what she had to say. "I haven't taken anything you bought me. I'm sorry about all the money you've spent on me, but I never asked you to do that. I know I accepted . . ." She shook her head. "There's nothing I can do about it. I didn't plan to have a baby, no matter what you think. If you don't mind, I'll ring for a taxi to come and pick me up, and then . . ."

Her throat tightened, strangling the last fateful words. Tears pricked at her eyes. She swung around and picked up the telephone. Her hand was shaking. She tried to read the number but her eyes were blurred and the little figures swam indistinctly.

"God damn it, Eden!" The telephone receiver was snatched out of her hand and crashed onto its stand. She was swung around. Strong hands gripped her upper arms, fingers digging into her soft flesh. "Do you think I'd turn you out into the street with nothing? I know you once called me a monster, but I'm not that monstrous!''

There was a strain of appalled horror in his voice, but Eden couldn't bear to look at him. She closed her eyes. Her throat ached too much to speak. Her heart was twisted in pure agony. She heard Luke mutter something savage under his breath. Then he pulled her with him to a kitchen chair and sat her at the small breakfast table.

''There's got to be a way out of this,'' he growled.

Eden was shaking too much to get up again. Luke swung away from her to the kitchen sink. She heard the tap run, then he was putting a glass of water in front of her.

''Drink it!'' he commanded.

She took a sip.

He placed a clean handkerchief beside her.

She wiped her eyes.

He paced up and down the kitchen floor, clenching and unclenching his hands until she had recovered some composure.

Eden knew in her heart that there was no way out of the trap she was in. Their relationship was irrevocably changed. Nothing could restore it to what it had been. Yet she couldn't find the strength to fight Luke's will. Eventually he would let her go, she thought dully. When the talking was done.

''You said you were taking precautions,'' he shot at her accusingly.

''Yes.''

''So how did it happen, Eden?''

''Before then. The night of Marlee's wedding.''

He wheeled around in shock. She could almost see the calculations going on in his brain. "That's four months!"

"Yes."

Silence. Thick, oppressive silence. She knew he was remembering back. The time she was supposed to have a period, the gradual thickening of her figure, so many little things that now took on new meaning to him. He looked sick.

"You've been living a lie with me for months," he said coldly.

"Yes."

"Why, Eden?"

"Because I wanted to stay with you."

"To get as much out of me as you could?" he asked with a hard edge of bitterness.

She stared blankly at him for several moments as disbelief faded into painful resignation. Her eyes dropped to her hands. They were still trembling. Stupid, she thought. She made herself shrug.

"If you want to think of me like that," she said flatly, "then I can't stop you from thinking like that." It didn't matter what he thought any more. It was finished. This was only prolonging the agony of ending it.

"I don't know what the hell to think!" he exploded vehemently. "Tell me, Eden!"

She lifted bleak black eyes to the burning blue of his. "I guess I was greedy for what we had together, Luke. I knew it would end as soon as you found out I was pregnant."

"Lies and deception. And I thought you were one woman who was honest," he said in disgust.

Eden flushed. Maybe she had been wrong not to tell him straight away, but he hadn't suffered all the agony

of mind she had been through because of his fair warning. He had got what *he* wanted throughout her painful dishonesty. Her eyes flashed fiery resentment of his
judgement of her.

"I thought I was giving you something in return for
all you've given me, Luke. How would you have felt if
I'd told you I was pregnant only a few weeks after you'd
made your—your investment in our living together?
Would you really have liked that *honesty*? Wouldn't
you have felt cheated?"

"I don't care about the money," he bit out angrily.
"I cared about—" he shook his head in dark anguish
"—about being able to trust you," he finished flatly.

"If that was the only important thing to you, then
I'm sorry for letting you down," she said. A deadly fa-
tigue washed through her, overwhelming the brief surge
of resentment. "I didn't like lying to you," she said
wearily. "A little bit of me died every time I did it. In a
way, I'm glad that part of it is over. At least now I can
be myself again."

A muscle in his jaw flinched. Uncertainty flickered in
his eyes. He turned aside and paced up and down some
more, his face grim. He shook his head. Words dragged
reluctantly from his lips. He did not look at her as he
spoke. He obviously didn't want to look at someone
who was carrying a child he didn't care for.

"I can't blame you for what happened on the night
of Marlee's wedding. You were...deeply disturbed. I
knew it, and I shouldn't have let myself be drawn into
what I did. It simply didn't occur to me that you..." He
grimaced. "Most single women are on the pill these
days. But I should have asked. Should have taken care."

"It was more my fault than yours," Eden said with a heavy sigh. "Forget it, Luke. It simply doesn't matter how it happened. It doesn't change anything."

He slashed her a hard, accusing look. "You've had more time to think about it."

"Yes," she snapped, impatient with the guilt he was laying on her. "And may I say I'd have preferred not to. If you think it's been fun for me, Luke, you can think again."

"All right!" he snapped back, then dragged in a deep breath. "I can see it was an accident."

"Big of you!"

Her sarcasm drew a glare from him. "That still doesn't excuse all your damned lies!"

"You can't have everything your own way, Luke," she bit out angrily. "You wanted me, but you didn't want me with a baby. Well, you got what you wanted! And now that I'm having a baby, I'm removing the terrible offence from your sight. I'm sorry it ended up a short-term investment for you, but you got a bad break. Tough luck! It's even tougher luck on me, but I realise you don't appreciate that. Nevertheless, I don't have to stay here and take any more of this—this persecution from you."

She pushed her chair back to stand up.

"Okay!" He waved her to stay seated. His blue eyes reinforced the command, pinning her in her chair with blazing intensity. "You're right. The fact of what's happened has to be faced. I'm getting there."

"Well, bully for you!" Eden said bitterly. "Let's see now. We've got past the emotional blackmail, entrapment, lies and deception. I suppose I should be grateful that you didn't accuse me of infidelity besides. Or are we still coming to that?"

He actually paused and considered. She saw the doubt flicker across his face and could hardly believe her eyes. To Eden, it was the final and utterly fatal stab to her love for him. For Luke to believe, even for a moment, that she might be carrying some other man's child damned him forever in her sight.

She stared at him with black condemnation and cold death in her heart. She saw him pull himself back from the brink of that unforgiveable accusation, but it didn't redeem him. He *had* thought it. He composed an apologetic expression and forced himself to meet her watching eyes.

"I'm sorry, Eden." He heaved a long sigh. "I wasn't prepared for this. I appreciate that my attitude made the situation difficult for you." The blue eyes burned with hard resolution. "I'm sorry I didn't respond in a more sympathetic manner. I hadn't planned for such an outcome to our living together."

"Neither did I!"

His surprise was almost comical. "You can't leave, Eden," he protested insistently.

"Can't I?" She rose to her feet, her spine stiff, her head high. "Remember the terms you laid out to me, Luke? Apart from the no marriage and the no children?"

He frowned heavily at her.

She stretched her mouth into a semblance of a smile. "You said I could walk out of our arrangement anytime I like. That time is now, Luke. I was merely giving you the courtesy of knowing why."

She turned her back on him and stepped towards the telephone.

"Wait!"

"There's nothing to wait for, Luke," she tossed at him, and once again picked up the telephone receiver to call for a taxi.

"Stop it, Eden!" There was a low throb of urgency in his voice. Stupidly it made her hesitate. Then he was around the table and taking the receiver out of her hand again. "You know you don't want to go. Any more than I want you to go. You wouldn't have lied to stay with me this long if you wanted to leave me," he argued with considerable passion.

It was a bad mistake—to refer to her *lies*. But then he made a worse mistake. He tried to draw Eden into an embrace. She recoiled from him in fierce rejection.

"Don't touch me, Luke!" she cried in anguish and despair. "Don't ever touch me again!" She snatched her handbag off the kitchen counter and backed away from him, black eyes glaring intense bitterness.

He looked bewildered. "For God's sake, Eden! I wasn't going to hurt you. I wanted—"

"*You* wanted!" she spat out. Her face worked through a number of uncontrollable emotions, but her eyes were steady, stabbing him as surely as he had stabbed her. "It's all been about what *you* want, Luke. I gave you the chance to show that you care about me. You'll never know how desperately I needed you to take me in your arms and say it was all right when I told you I was pregnant. But you didn't. All you cared about, all you thought about was *yourself*. And how I'd let you down."

He went white. One arm jerked out to her in appeal. "Eden . . ."

She shook her head vehemently. "You let *me* down, Luke. And I don't want you anywhere near me any more."

"For God's sake! You landed this on me out of the blue! But I do care about you, Eden. And if you're having my child, you can't—"

"If!" A high, cracked laugh issued from her throat. Her eyes glittered with wild primitive scorn. "I'll make it easy for you, Luke. Maybe Jeff flew back from Perth the weekend before Marlee's wedding. Maybe he came the week after, to try and make up with me. But by then I knew I had you. You can think that, Luke. It gives you the freedom to wipe me out of your life without another thought."

She laughed bitterly at him as conflicting emotions raged across his face. Then she swung on her heel and marched out of the kitchen and along the walkway to the elevator. Luke didn't try to stop her this time. Nor did he call out after her. She would have ignored him if he had. But he didn't.

She rode the elevator down to the entrance foyer of the apartment building and marched out to the street. As luck would have it, a taxi was dropping off a couple of passengers right in front of her. The driver was only too happy to pick up another fare straight away. Eden settled onto the back seat, gave the driver her Glebe address, and the car shot off up the road, away from Luke Selby and towards a life without him.

No prizes for Eden, she thought bitterly. Life is a blank, empty space. Adversity was her lot. She might as well accept that and get on with fighting it, making the best of what was possible. She had been a blind stupid fool to let herself love Luke Selby. Marlee had been right. A dead end to dreams.

She felt a funny little lurch in her stomach. Her hand instinctively moved there to cover the place. Another odd, fleeting ripple. A sense of awe gripped Eden's mind. Her baby moving? Was that what it was? The life inside her stirring, letting her know she was not alone?

The thought gave Eden a strange peace of mind. Whatever the future held for her and her child, they would have each other. They would not be alone.

CHAPTER ELEVEN

EDEN WOKE LATE the next morning. She lay in the narrow single bed, which sagged in the middle, and let her gaze rove slowly around her new surroundings. No view of Sydney Harbour. No garden terrace. No loving man beside her. This was the present. And the future, until she could afford something better.

At least it was not a poky little room. She did have a fair amount of space to move around in. The battered-looking wardrobe was more than big enough to hold her clothes. The chest of drawers beside her bed was handy for her tape deck. The table under the window was a fair size. The two accompanying chairs were little more than serviceable, but there was one comfortable armchair for reading and relaxing. No television, of course.

Her four pot-plants lent a personal touch to the room, giving it a bit of much-needed colour. The iron-grey Axminster carpet was dull and well-worn, giving little comfort underfoot, and the walls were painted a washed-out salmony shade. Glue marks and brighter squares of paint on the wall showed where posters had been hung by Eden's predecessor. I'll get some posters, Eden thought.

The curtains and the bedspread were of the same heavy-duty cotton, patterned in geometric shapes of dark blue and grey, with thin outlines of pinky-beige and white. The fabric had also been used to upholster the one armchair. It wasn't a bad room at all, Eden told herself. She could have done a lot worse in the circumstances.

There were no bookshelves. She had pushed her boxes of books under the bed. They could stay there, she thought. Bookshelves cost money she could not afford.

Before she started work at Ray's office she had to buy some new clothes—maternity clothes. Nothing really fit any more. Not even her old stretch jeans could be done up at the waist.

At least the morning sickness had eased off, Eden thought gratefully as she pushed herself out of bed. Her bathroom was very basic—washbasin, shower, toilet—but at least it was her own, and it served its purpose. There was only one mirror, on the door of the little cupboard over the washbasin. That was fine by Eden, too. She didn't want to look at the changes in her figure. It was bad enough looking at her face, which was pasty this morning and showing dark shadows under her eyes.

She washed and dressed and went out to the communal kitchen. There she had one cupboard assigned to her, which she could keep locked. She was supposed to write her name on anything she put in the refrigerator and freezer. Eden got out the breakfast cereal and the milk she had brought the previous day and sat down at the laminated table provided for meals. None of the occupants of the other three bed-sits came by while she ate her breakfast. All gone about their business for the day, she reasoned.

A red pay phone on the wall near the door drew her attention. She should call Marlee, Eden thought, let her know that the break with Luke had been effected.

Marlee would be upset if she rang Luke's apartment and found Eden gone without leaving any means for letting her get in touch. She would worry. And that wouldn't be fair. Marlee was pregnant, too.

Eden washed her cereal bowl and spoon, put everything away, then fetched her handbag from her room. She needed to do some more food shopping, as well. Some fruit and other handy snacks that she could keep in her room. But she would call Marlee first.

The moment Eden announced herself on the telephone, Marlee burst into agitated speech. "Thank God! I've been so worried about you. Where are you now, Eden? Let me come and help."

Eden was momentarily stunned that Marlee already knew of her move. Which meant Luke must have told her. Bluntly, no doubt, and with no assurance that Eden had a place to go to, which was why Marlee was in a tizz.

"I'm fine, Marlee," Eden assured her in a strong, firm voice. "There's no reason for you to be upset. I'm settled in a nice, respectable bed-sit apartment, and I'll be ready to go to work at Ray's office when the time comes."

"You really have got a place, Eden?" Still an anxious, uncertain note. "You're not just telling me that?"

Eden's heart twisted. Her lies and pretending had also undermined Marlee's trust in her. "I promise you I have a decent place, Marlee," she said sadly.

A long, fraught pause. "I want to come and see you."

"Not today." Eden didn't want to talk about what had happened with Luke. "I'm very busy. I have a lot of shopping to do. I'll meet you for lunch next week when I've got myself better organised."

"Eden—" a deep sigh "—do you think you might have been too hasty in walking out on Luke?"

"No. I told you it had to be done, Marlee," Eden reminded her. "It's done."

"But, Eden—" Another deep sigh. "Luke came around here looking for you last night. At first he wouldn't believe that I didn't know where you were. He was... he was in a state, Eden. He went away and then came back again hours later, asking if you'd called me. He was distraught, Eden. He confessed that he'd reacted badly to your telling him about the baby and he wanted to make it right for you. He asked me to let him know where you were as soon as I knew."

He feels guilty, that's all, Eden thought savagely. "Well, you can tell him from me that I'm safe and well and I don't need him," she said tersely.

"Eden..." A pleading note.

"And tell him to stop pestering you, because you're my friend and you stand by me. That's if you still want to stand by me."

"Oh, Eden! Of course I do. And I will. It's just that... Well, I thought he did love you, Eden. And he said he would make it right for you," she argued gently.

"He can't! He had his chance, Marlee. There's no going back."

Make it right with money, Eden thought caustically. That was Luke's way of making everything right. Well, he couldn't buy an easy conscience from her with his damned money! She'd stood on her own two feet before she met him, and she'd do it again.

"You can tell him truthfully that you don't know where I am, because you don't," she said with angry vehemence.

"Eden..."

She quickly tempered her tone, wanting to soothe her friend's concern. "It's best this way, Marlee, believe me! And you mustn't worry about me. I'm fine. I'll call you next week about meeting for lunch. Just don't talk to me about Luke. Ever again. I never want to hear his name."

She hung up and found herself trembling so much she had to sit down for a while. Eventually she gathered herself together and went shopping. Several times she had to snap herself out of staring blankly at goods on the supermarket shelves. Once another shopper paused to ask her if she was all right. Eden assured her she was only thinking. But she wasn't. She was hardly thinking at all. It was much better not to think.

That evening she met her new neighbours. All girls, much to Eden's relief. The girls were students doing tertiary education courses, which they hoped would lead them into good careers. At their inquiry, Eden said she was about to start work in an accounting firm, which sounded too dull to provoke any further interest.

Eden was particularly drawn to a cheerful, perky girl whose mobile face was vibrantly expressive. Her name was Kate Reid. She was tall and thin—probably from all the energy she burned up, Eden thought, because she certainly wasn't dieting on the pizza she ate for dinner. She had an unruly mop of carrot-red hair and hazel eyes that danced with sharp intelligence.

"I'm in my last year at the College of Arts," she told Eden. "Fabric and dress design."

"And one of these days she's going to have her own label and be famous," another of the girls put in laughingly. "Aren't you, Kate?"

"You can laugh on the other side of your face when I make the big time and you can't afford to buy my label," Kate retorted good-humouredly.

Eden thought of Paula Michaelson and hastily pushed the image of those clothes out of her mind. They were in the past. Nothing to do with her future. Yet when Kate asked Eden if she would like to see her work, Eden agreed that she would, thinking that any distraction was better than being alone with her thoughts. She instinctively liked Kate. Maybe the girl would become a friend.

Kate's bed-sit was a revelation as to what could be done with a room. She had designed her own fabrics to dress up her surroundings, and they were a symphony of greens and purple and yellow. Apart from the sewing machine sitting at one end, her table was piled high with folders of designs that all looked fabulous to Eden.

"You're very talented!" Eden exclaimed admiringly as she leafed through the sketches.

Kate gave a wry smile. "Talent, but no capital to go into business for myself. But I've scraped myself up from the gutter this far, and I'll make it to the top one day. Watch me."

"Where have you come from?" Eden questioned sympathetically.

It transpired that Kate had had as poor and as underprivileged a background as Eden, and they soon fell into a sympathetic swapping of life stories. Except, of course, for Eden's interlude with Luke. However, she saw no point in holding back what would soon become obvious, so she confessed to Kate that she was four months pregnant.

"I take it the father doesn't want to know about it," Kate remarked cynically.

"No. He didn't," Eden answered briefly.

"Like my father. Take the pleasure, leave the pain." Kate sat glumly for a few moments. Then her face lit with an ecstatic smile. "Tell you what, Eden. I could design you some maternity clothes. Make you look hardly pregnant at all. We could go shopping for fabrics this weekend and have ourselves a ball. What do you say? It'd save you a lot of money," she added appealingly.

"But, Kate, I can't..." Her glance at the sewing machine betrayed her thought before she spoke it.

"I'll run them up for you in no time flat. I'm a wizard on that machine," Kate boasted.

"Only if you let me pay you, Kate," Eden protested.

"Are you a good cook?" Kate asked.

Eden was bewildered by the irrelevant question. "Yes. But what..."

"Tell you what. I love home-cooked meals but I'm no good at cooking. You cook me a proper dinner every so often, and we'll be all square," Kate declared.

"That's too one-sided," Eden protested.

"No argument. This will be good experience for me. Maybe I'll work up a special maternity line. You'll make a great model, Eden. You look so beautiful, photographers will be lining up in the street to capture shots of maternity in bloom."

Eden had to laugh, but there were a few emotional tears mixed with her laughter.

"Deal?" Kate pressed.

"Deal," Eden agreed. "And thank you, Kate."

Kate wrinkled her nose in a funny, self-mocking expression. "It's just that I thrive on admiration, and good cooking."

"I'll cook you the best meals you've ever eaten," Eden promised.

Kate Reid was a godsend to Eden. How she would have coped without the enlivening friendship and companionship of the other girl, she didn't know. Concocting special dinners and discussing the art of fashion design kept her mind well occupied in the hours that weren't taken up by the business course she resumed the following week.

Not only that, but when she did meet Marlee for lunch, she had something cheerful to talk about. She was conscious of her friend watching her like a hawk, apparently unconvinced that Eden's heart wasn't broken. Although Marlee did not speak a word about Luke, Eden felt him there like a ghost at a feast, the unspoken presence haunting them both. She knew that her gaiety sounded brittle, but Marlee—God bless her!—played along with being cheerful and forward-looking. Except her eyes knew too much.

Eden came away from the meeting with her dearest friend, wondering if they would ever be able to get over the barrier that her association with Luke had unwittingly created. If only Marlee's husband wasn't Luke's brother... Yet Ray was everything Marlee wanted, and Eden could not begrudge her friend's happiness in her marriage. Time would resolve the problem, she told herself.

The day finally came when Eden was to begin her job in Ray's office. She wore Kate's navy and white creation, a suit cleverly cut and designed to give Eden ample room to bloom, as Kate put it, but which was so smart no-one would class it as maternity. It gave Eden confidence that she would not look at all out of place in a business office.

When she gave her name at the reception desk, the girl there knew she was expected, and after a minute or two, Ray himself came to greet her and take her to where she was to work. He introduced her to the woman whose place she was to take when she left in a week's time. The woman was several years older than Eden, and eight months pregnant. She very kindly explained all the work procedures Eden would have to carry out, then supervised while Eden did her best to master everything.

By the end of her first day, Eden was satisfied that she would be able to cope with the job. Ray dropped by her desk just as she was packing up to go. He had a look of nervous concern on his face. Which was only natural, Eden reasoned. After all, he had more or less given her the job because of her friendship with Marlee.

"How did today go?" he asked.

"It's okay, Ray," she assured him. "I can do it."

He gave her a strained smile. "I didn't have much doubt about that, Eden. Marlee says you can do anything you set your mind to."

Eden laughed. "Marlee is a little prejudiced on my behalf. But I promise I won't let you down, Ray."

For some reason that remark made him ill at ease. His eyes searched hers. "I hope you understand that Marlee and I do have your interests at heart, Eden. You won't forget that, will you?"

"Of course I won't, Ray," Eden said sincerely. "I'm very grateful to you for this chance."

He shrugged off her gratitude. "Anything we can do, just let us know, Eden. Marlee would be very upset if you . . . cut her off, Eden."

"I'd never do that, Ray," Eden said quickly, shocked that he would think that of her.

He nodded. "That's okay then," he said with a troubling note of uncertainty.

Have I upset Marlee? Eden wondered as she watched Ray retreat to his office. Does she feel cut off by me? It nagged at Eden's conscience as she rode the elevator to the ground floor. I'll call her as soon as I get home, she determined. After all, Marlee would want to know about her first day at work.

Ray's firm of accountants was situated in a huge office building in the inner city. People were streaming across the entrance foyer when Eden emerged from her elevator. All hurrying home, Eden thought. It was a novelty to her to be part of this kind of crowd, so she didn't hurry. It felt strange to have her work over for the day at five o'clock in the afternoon.

As she passed through the revolving doors to the street, she felt another rippling movement from her baby. She halted on the pavement outside, her hand sliding under her loose-fitting navy jacket to cover her stomach, hoping the baby would move again. It did a few seconds later. A private little smile lit her face. Then someone bumped her in passing by and she realised she was blocking the pedestrian traffic by standing still.

She looked up...and there was Luke directly in front of her, watching her, waiting to catch her attention. A wave of heat burst through her body, tingling to her toes and burning across her cheeks. She whipped her head around, evading the treacherous magnetism of the naked and hungry desire in the blue eyes. She forced her legs to turn her body away from him, to walk towards the bus-stop in the next street.

It came to her through a fog of renewed pain that this was what Ray had been uncomfortable about. He had betrayed her to his brother. And Marlee? Had Marlee agreed to this?

"Eden!" Harsh urgency in Luke's voice, scraping over all the wounds he had scored on her vulnerable heart.

She kept her gaze fixed directly ahead, ignoring him, but he fell into step beside her. Her heart felt as though it was catapulting around her chest. Go away, go away, she silently begged, hating him for breaking into her new life, just when she had it all set up to move forward without looking back.

"Eden, I'm going to talk to you," he said, sounding grimly determined.

She stared stonily ahead. "I don't want anything from you, Luke. We have nothing to talk about," she stated decisively.

"Then listen!" he demanded.

"I don't want to listen. I didn't like what I heard last time. Please leave me alone." She listened to her heels clacking along the pavement. Almost at the corner. Another thirty metres and she would be at the bus-stop.

"I don't blame you for feeling the way you do, but I swear it will be different this time, Eden," he said vehemently.

She flashed him a scathing look. "How can it be, with your attitudes?"

Looking at him was a mistake. She quickly jerked her head forward but his face was left imprinted on her mind. The face that had lain on the pillow beside hers for so many nights and mornings, the face she had loved. And the pained blue eyes pleading for her forbearance. What did he want of her now? Couldn't he see it was impossible?

"I was wrong!"

That admission gave her pause for thought. Curiosity got the better of her. "About what?" she asked.

"About everything."

Too sweeping a generality. Eden didn't believe it. Luke was far too self-assured to think he was wrong about everything. Yet a moment ago he hadn't looked self-assured. He had looked ... desperate.

"I'm sorry for the way I reacted that night, Eden," he went on in a low voice that throbbed with feeling. "It was stupid and destructive and I regret it very deeply."

"It was what you felt," she dismissed harshly, not wanting to remember that night. Keep walking and don't look at him again, she told herself.

"It hasn't been what I've felt since then," he argued. "We were good together, Eden. You can't deny that."

"It was a fool's dream, Luke."

"I love you."

Her feet faltered. She pushed them forward again, ignoring the pain in her heart. What she would have given to have heard that from him when it really counted! "No, you don't," she said with bitter certainty. "You don't know what love is about, Luke."

"I know my life isn't worth living without you, Eden."

"You are forgetting one little item, aren't you?" she rushed out with withering sarcasm, fighting hard to stop herself from wanting to be with him again. It could never be the same, she told herself savagely. "It isn't only me anymore," she added, to nail the point home to him as well as herself.

"I want the child, too," he said in a soft, strained voice.

Her stomach contracted. She stopped dead. It was a lie, her mind dictated. It had to be a lie. He couldn't mean it. Not after all he'd said. Besides, the fact that he'd never bothered being a father to his other child damned him on that score.

"Eden . . ."

"No!" She shook her head vehemently. "I won't listen to you! I won't!"

Her legs felt like wooden blocks but she got them moving. Around the corner. Her bus was at the stop. A queue of passengers were boarding. Frantic to get away from the man who was tormenting her with false promises, she ran forward and made it to the bus in time to follow the last person on board. The effort made her dizzy. She was breathing hard. Her heart seemed to be pounding in her ears. She struggled along the aisle to a vacant seat and gratefully subsided onto it, closing her eyes in abject relief.

She felt someone slide onto the seat beside her. She automatically crammed herself closer to the window, recoiling from any human contact, but she did not open her eyes. She concentrated hard on stopping the trembling that kept rippling through her. The bus made several stops before she managed to get herself under control.

"Eden . . ."

Her eyes flew open in shock. That soft voice belonged to Luke. She hadn't left him behind at all. He was sitting beside her!

"Why are you doing this to me?" she cried despairingly. "It's no good, Luke."

"I want the chance to put my case to you."

She gave a harsh, derisive laugh. "You don't have to be fair to me, but I have to be fair to you. That's typical!"

"I want to be fair to you."

She turned her head and stared out the window. Her whole body felt in upheaval. A flood of bitterness put a sour taste in her mouth. He had been unfair from the very beginning, pursuing her when he knew he wouldn't offer her any of her dreams. The only rule Luke lived by was what *he wanted*.

"How do you intend to be fair to me this time, Luke?" she asked wearily.

There was a brief silence, then very softly, "Will you marry me, Eden?"

CHAPTER TWELVE

Eden looked sharply at Luke, unsure that she had heard right. The blue eyes locked onto hers, compelling in their intense purpose, striking at her heart like claws that would drag her his way. She tore her gaze from his and stared blindly out the window again.

Marriage!

A loving husband and happy children and a good solid home and a beautiful garden... The dreams rose up again and flowered briefly in her mind. But everything she knew about Luke told her that such images were pipe dreams that could not eventuate with him.

No risks, no prizes...

Luke's catchphrase taunted her self-protective caution. But Luke was a bad risk. A bad, bad risk. This proposal, against all his personal principles and values, was the only path left to him to ease his conscience about her. His sense of responsibility insisted on looking after her while she had his child.

Then would come the pain. Luke didn't want anything to do with children. He wouldn't want to share in their child. He would resent the time she spent on it, and she would end up torn between the two of them. What happiness could there be in that? Marriage to Luke simply wouldn't work. It couldn't work.

"You said you'd never go down that road again, Luke," she reminded him flatly.

"I want to with you, Eden."

"Because of the baby?" she mocked.

"No. Because I want you with me always. Because I don't want to spend the rest of my life without you. Because your happiness is my happiness, Eden, and I was a fool to wipe out marriage with you in the first place."

He sounded sincere. Passionately sincere. But he was leaving out the baby as though it didn't exist and would have no bearing on their existence. She took a deep breath and shook her head.

"Thank you for the offer, Luke..."

"But the answer is no?"

"That's right."

"Why?"

"Because for the rest of your life you'll think I forced you into this marriage. One day you'll say it. And that will be the end."

"That won't happen."

"Yes, it will," Eden said sadly. "I'm having a baby you don't want. There can't be any trust between us any more. Remember all my lies to you. Making an *honest* woman of me doesn't repair that, Luke."

"Eden, I realise I gave you no choice but to hide that knowledge from me as long as you could," he said in soft apology. "I'm bitterly sorry for forcing you into such a painful dilemma, and then blaming you for what you did. Believe me, I'll give you no reason for needing to hide anything from me again. Give me the chance to prove that to you, Eden."

Temptation swirled around her mind. Her heart beat faster in its eagerness to grasp the chance he was holding out to her. But Luke was so good with words.

Hadn't he argued her into living with him, against all her convictions and principles?

He was carefully evading the issue of the baby, concentrating on her, knowing how much she had wanted him, knowing how much she had debased all she believed in simply to stay with him. She had paid *his* price, and now he was offering to pay *her* price, but did he really accept it in his heart? Would he fling it in her face the moment things started to go wrong between them? Which would undoubtedly happen once the baby was born.

Probably before then.

Kate's navy and white suit successfully disguised her pregnancy so that she looked the same to Luke today, but she couldn't imagine that he would find her so desirable when she got distended out of shape. Even in the weeks since she had left him her condition had become far more obvious in her naked state. If he showed any sign of distaste... No, she couldn't bear that reaction from him. Whichever way she looked at it, the baby was going to separate them, so it was far less wear and tear on her emotions to effect the separation now.

"No," she said. "I can get along fine on my own. It's better that way. I can't cope with you, Luke. It would tear me apart again."

"Eden, let me explain to you about my first marriage."

He certainly hadn't stuck with that, Eden thought. "What happened with some other woman has nothing to do with you and me, Luke. I'm a different person to your ex-wife. You lived with me for almost four months, and yet—" a hard bitter look "—you doubted my word that the child is yours."

He paled. "Eden, please, if you'll let me explain..."

The bus was slowing down, approaching her stop. Eden swung around to face him, her black eyes fierce with rejection. "No matter what you say, I'll never forget that, Luke. This is the end of the road." She struggled to her feet. "I'm getting off now, and I don't want you to come any farther with me."

He looked ill, his face tight and bleak, the blue eyes pained and lifeless. "I'm sorry," he said in a low, hollow voice.

He moved to stand up in the aisle and let her out. People looked at him. He was so strikingly handsome in his expensive banker's clothes. Heads turned to look at her, as well. Eden flushed with embarrassment as she realised that her highly personal conversation with Luke must have been overheard by the passengers around them.

Luke touched her arm as she was about to brush past him. "If you are ever in need of anything, please call on me, Eden," he said softly. "And those are not pious words. I do mean them."

She hesitated, her heart twisting with dark anguish. She loved him, still loved him, but that didn't change anything. She remembered the child of his first marriage, whom he had virtually disowned. The child in her womb wouldn't fare any better with him. It was no use wanting what couldn't be.

"Goodbye, Luke," she said huskily.

She pushed herself forward to make a quick exit as the bus ground to a halt. She was painfully conscious that Luke was not following her. Had he finally accepted that this was the end of the road for them?

As she stepped down to the pavement, it occurred to her that it was probably a mistake to get out of the bus here. It revealed the general area of where she lived. But Ray could tell Luke her exact address anyway. She had written it down on the employment form she had filled in this morning.

Ray and Marlee. No doubt they thought they did have her best interests at heart in trying to bring her and Luke together again. Particularly if he'd told them he was prepared to offer marriage. Eden couldn't blame Marlee for thinking it was the answer to everything. Luke could be very convincing.

The bus pulled away, faces at the windows looking at her with both curious and frustrated interest. Luke was still standing in the aisle where she had left him, watching her with an expression of sick hungry yearning that curled around her soul, tugging at it unmercifully. Then there was only the back of the bus, blanking him out, taking him away from her.

You have a place of your own, she told herself. Go there. One step after another, mechanical movement, heart pumping intense distress, mind blank. Eden had no recollection of the distance she walked to the front gate of the big ugly building that housed her little apartment. Suddenly she was there.

She looked up. No architectural pretensions about this building. It was a double-storeyed slab of a house in reinforced concrete, painted the same salmon-pink colour as the interior walls. The colour had probably been an industrial special when the old house had been renovated into its present bed-sit apartments, four up, four down. The communal laundry was an addition at the back of the house.

There was no garden, front or back. The front gate led straight onto a concrete porch, which was only wide enough to shelter the front door, and the small back yard was similarly concreted. No doubt it saved any problems about maintenance.

Nothing about it could compare to the way Luke lived, but at least it was clean and respectable, Eden assured herself. Glebe was an old suburb—one of the oldest in Sydney—but it wasn't a slum area. Her child would have a better start in life than she had had, and it would have all the love and care and protection and security that she could give it.

She pushed open the gate and went inside. Her bedsit was on the upper floor. As she reached the top of the stairs Kate Reid popped out of her room and greeted her with a cheerful grin.

"Hi! How did it go?"

It drew a wry smile from Eden. "The job went well. And no-one seemed to notice that I was pregnant."

"Ha!" said Kate triumphantly. "Smart design, wasn't it?"

"Very smart," Eden agreed.

"You must be tired," Kate said sympathetically, then grinned again. "Cook's night off. I'm meeting some friends down at Enzio's. We're going to pig out on Italian food. Want to join us? You can stuff yourself on good, filling pasta for about ten dollars."

Eden hesitated. She had no appetite at all, and the money could better be spent on other things. Yet the thought of being alone in that little cheerless room tonight, the meeting with Luke all too ready to prey on her mind and heart, was persuasion enough that the extravagance would be worthwhile. At least she would have distracting company.

She nodded. "I'd like that."

"Leaving in ten minutes. I'll knock on your door."

Eden struggled through the evening, forcing food down her throat, smiling at Kate's friends, trying hard to listen to their gay chatter and respond when necessary. By the time she returned to her bed-sit she was mercifully tired enough to go straight to sleep.

She saw nothing of Ray at work the next day. Luke was not waiting for her when she finally emerged from the office building. Definitely the end of the road, she told herself, sternly ignoring the unhappy regrets in her heart. The bus trip home was uneventful. She cooked Kate a Chinese recipe with stir-fried chicken. Kate rolled her eyes and smacked her lips in ecstasy. It raised Eden's spirits a little.

However, Kate had college work to do, and when Eden went to her lonely room, no matter how hard she tried to keep depression at bay, it rolled over her. She wished she had a television. She was going through her tapes to find some uplifting music to play when there was a knock on her door. Thinking it was Kate to tell her something or other, Eden was totally surprised when she opened the door to find Marlee standing there.

Her small face looked strained and sombre. Her lovely amber eyes searched Eden's uncertainly, as though unsure of a welcome. Eden smiled and threw her arms around her friend in an impulsive hug, letting her know there were no hard feelings about the betrayal to Luke. Never would she cut Marlee off from her friendship or affection.

Yet strangely Marlee did not return Eden's hug. She stood stiffly in her embrace. Eden drew back, frowning. "Is something wrong, Marlee?" she asked in concern.

"Yes. Very wrong," Marlee replied. "May I come in?"

"Of course." Eden quickly stepped into the room and waved her inside. "It's nothing grand but it's good enough for me," she added. There was something about Marlee's demeanour that made her feel defensive. Which was odd, because she had never felt that way with Marlee before. She shut the door and gestured towards the armchair. "Take a seat."

In expectation of Marlee's accepting the invitation, Eden moved over to her bed and perched herself on it, hoping for a long heart-to-heart talk. But Marlee did not sit down. She stood in front of the table, staring at Eden as though she was confronting a stranger.

"I've come to say goodbye to you, Eden," she announced in a low, strained voice.

"What do you mean?" Eden asked, feeling more and more unsettled by Marlee's manner. "Are you and Ray going somewhere?"

"We've been through everything together, haven't we, Eden?" There was a look of hurt accusation in Marlee's eyes.

"Yes, we have," Eden agreed softly, realising that this had to be something very serious.

"We've stood beside each other—"

"Like sisters."

Marlee shifted from foot to foot, her inner agitation obviously building. "You've done something terribly, terribly wrong," she burst out in hurt protest.

"What on earth are you talking about?" Eden cried in bewilderment and concern.

"I never thought you were like that, Eden. I thought I knew you through and through."

"Marlee?" Eden was shocked. She lifted her hands in helpless appeal. "What have I done?"

"You're punishing Luke for hurting you. Making him pay for not living up to your dreams when *you* wanted him to," she said fiercely. "You're not being fair to either Luke or your child. And I never thought you could be like that."

Eden stiffened. "You don't know what went on between us, Marlee."

"Yes, I do. Enough to know you're wrong, Eden. Terribly, selfishly wrong!"

"Me, selfish?" Eden could hardly believe Marlee was talking to her like this. "You think *I'm* being selfish?"

"Yes! You lived with Luke because you loved him. Or so you said. I believed you, Eden. Even when you should have told him about the baby, I let myself believe that you knew best. I've always trusted your judgement. But I couldn't help thinking it was wrong. Because there should be trust between two people who love each other. You didn't give Luke the chance to show he loved you enough to understand what had happened and work things out between you. You were unfair. You were selfish. And you were wrong!"

"He got his chance, Marlee," Eden reminded her tightly.

"After you'd lied and lied to him," Marlee shot back at her. "You can't blame him for reacting badly in those circumstances."

"You don't understand—"

"I understand that Luke came to me and Ray that night, totally distraught at having driven you away from him. You demanded that I stand by your decision not to let Luke know where you were. Out of loyalty to you, I did that, Eden."

Marlee began to shake. Her amber eyes burned with accusation. Eden had never seen her friend like this before. She was shaken by the passion of Marlee's speech. She was even more shaken by what her friend said.

"I did that for you while I watched a man who loved you go through hell because of it. Luke kept coming around to us, hoping for some contact with you. He begged me to tell him your dreams. He took me out with him in search of a house that might suit you. A house with enough grounds so that you could have your garden. He wanted to give you everything you wanted. We found it last weekend... the kind of house you always talked about, Eden, with verandas all around and lots of room for children to play. Luke put a holding deposit on it. And then I couldn't stand by you any more. So I told him about you starting work for Ray."

Tears glittered in her eyes. "It was wrong not to give him a chance. He loves you. He loves you so much..." She bit her lips, unable to go on while she struggled to contain her emotion.

"But the baby..." It was a ragged little protest from Eden. Faced with what Luke had done for her, she did not know what to think anymore. Her insides were churning.

"Luke wants the baby!" Marlee burst out vehemently.

"But his first child..."

"Ask him about it!"

"How can I?"

"He gave you the opportunity. He'll give you another one. He'll give you anything!"

Eden shook her head. "This is none of your business, Marlee."

"I can't stand letting you do this to yourself and your baby. It's a dreadful mistake. You didn't let Luke think about the baby long enough, Eden. Then yesterday, when he wanted to explain to you, you wouldn't listen. I know he hurt you. But, for heaven's sake! You hurt him, too. He wants to make up for it and you won't let him. And if you stay like that..."

The tears brimmed over her lashes and started spilling down her cheeks. Eden lurched to her feet, hands reaching out to her friend.

Marlee backed away towards the door, her own hands held out in rejection and a deeply distressed denial. "I don't want to know you anymore," she sobbed. "You're not the Eden I knew and loved. You've turned into someone else. And—and..." She burst into violent sobs and ran out of the room, banging the door behind her.

Eden stood there as though turned to stone, too shocked to move. Marlee rejecting their friendship after all these years, taking Luke's side against her. A feeling of bereftness and betrayal seared her soul. She had lost the only two people she had ever loved.

Was it her fault?

But what about the child Luke already had?

Could he explain away the terrible indifference, the desertion of a child he had fathered?

Even if everything Marlee said was true—and Eden couldn't disbelieve her—how could Luke rationalise such an action on his part?

I should have listened.

The words played through Eden's mind again and again, pricking her conscience until she could not bear the weight of guilt that built up inside her. Marlee was right. She had been wrong. Terribly, and yes, selfishly, wrong. She had lied to Luke to safeguard her happiness with him. She had rationalised it away by insisting to herself that it was for Luke too, but mainly it had been her own need for him that she had fed with her lies. She had become a stranger, even to herself.

And she had blamed Luke for it. Blamed him and punished him for not trusting her, when she had tarnished the trust he'd had in her. She had taken a holier-than-thou attitude and not forgiven him for the mistakes he had made. He had forgiven her. He had shown more understanding than she'd shown him. She had refused to listen to him, refused to believe him when he said he loved her and he wanted the child, too.

There was only one thing to do.

The only right thing.

Luke had said she could call him if she was ever in need of anything. She was now. She needed him to tell her all the things she wouldn't listen to before. She needed to know if she was wrong, and how wrong she had been. She needed to make everything right . . . if it were possible.

The thought of Marlee . . . What had she done?

Moving numbly, she took the necessary coins out of her purse and went out to the pay phone. It would be the most difficult phone call she had ever made in her life.

CHAPTER THIRTEEN

THE REPETITIVE BUZZ of the connection tone seemed like a water torture in Eden's mind. Each ring sounded louder and more nerve-racking. Perhaps Luke wasn't home. He could be anywhere. Doing his best to forget her for a while. She couldn't blame him for that. Being alone opened the door to black depression. If Luke didn't answer...

The tormenting buzz was abruptly cut off. Luke's voice recited his telephone number in a dull, matter-of-fact tone. Eden took a deep breath in an attempt to calm her quivering nerves. It did not succeed. She could hear the tremulous note in her voice when she answered.

"Luke, it's Eden. Is it...is it convenient for me to talk to you?"

"Yes. Yes, of course," he said quickly, a half-incredulous note in his voice.

"I want to apologise for...for cutting you off as I did yesterday. I should have listened when you wanted to explain. It wasn't fair of me. And I wondered..." She hesitated, agonising over how to ask him for another chance.

"Eden, if there's anything you want, you have only to ask," he said softly.

Tears welled in her eyes. Luke had always been kind and generous. "Thank you," she said huskily. "I'd like to talk with you again, Luke, but not...not over the phone.''

"Now? If I come to you, Eden?"

"Yes. Please. If that's all right."

"Are you...at your place?" he asked.

"Yes. It's—"

"I know where it is, Eden. I'll be there in about fifteen minutes," he said briskly.

The click of disconnection came before she could thank him. The thought of Luke's coming threw Eden into more inner turmoil. She fumbled the phone back onto its wall bracket, then hurried to her room, half panicking at the thought that Luke would see it as a terribly comfortless place. She shouldn't have invited him here. Yet what had to be said shrieked out for privacy.

The room was tidy. She couldn't make it look any better. Then she thought of her own appearance and raced into the bathroom to wash her face of any stale make-up and brush her hair. She told herself it didn't matter what she looked like, but somehow it did. She was glad she still had on the red and black shift that she had worn to work. It was Kate's most striking design, and Eden had worn it today in an effort to cheer herself up.

As each minute passed, Eden grew more and more agitated, pacing around the room, trying to compose herself and her thoughts...hope, despair, a sick yearning for everything to turn out right.

When the knock finally came on her door, she felt positively ill from the force of her churning emotions. Only a sheer act of will moved her legs the necessary distance to open the door and admit the man who could make or break the happiness she so desperately wanted.

Her heart squeezed tight as she looked up at him, recognising the same desire in his eyes. "I'm glad you called, Eden," he said, his voice a low throb of suppressed emotion. Then, when she stood there hopelessly tongue-tied, he added, "May I come in?"

She swallowed to get rid of the constriction in her throat. "Yes. Please do," she managed stiffly.

He was wearing informal clothes, blue jeans and a royal blue sports shirt that was open-necked and short-sleeved. They seemed to emphasise his powerful physique, and Eden couldn't help remembering how he looked with no clothes at all. How he felt . . .

Her bones went weak. Her hand trembled as she shut the door. She sat down abruptly on the nearest of the two chairs at the table. Luke seemed to fill the room. She saw his gaze sweep quickly around her living space before he swung back to her. He drew out the other chair from the table.

"May I?" he asked before sitting.

She nodded.

He sat, leaning his forearms on the table. His fingers laced together, long, sensitive fingers that had caressed her so many times with love. Eden wrenched her gaze to his and forced her voice to work.

"Thank you for coming, Luke."

"I wanted to," he said with a soft half smile. His eyes said he wanted so much more, if she were willing.

Eden took a deep breath and plunged straight to the heart of the matter. "Yesterday you offered to tell me . . . about your life."

"Whatever you want to know," he said easily.

Eden didn't find the words easy to come by. It was such a terrible invasion of his privacy . . . of his soul. She forced herself to go on with what she had started.

"Luke, will you tell me... Will you please tell me... Tell me why you don't have anything to do with...with your other child?"

His smile turned into a grimace of distaste. Whatever he had been expecting, it wasn't this. The blue eyes flickered from hers for a moment, then came back with a steady, purposeful glint. "I've never told anybody that, Eden," he said quietly.

She rose from her chair, too agitated to sit still. Her hand moved instinctively to smooth down the red and black shift that hid her pregnancy. Our child, she thought in frantic need. What had happened with the other child was so important!

"Luke...if we are to get back together—" her eyes pleaded with him "—if there is any chance of us being happy together, I need to know."

He rose from his chair, his face tight, his hands clenching. "It's a matter of...pride."

Eden looked away, a sense of hopelessness ripping through her heart. "I shouldn't have asked."

"No. You have every right to ask," he said grimly.

Her eyes fluttered to him.

He looked away. His gaze seemed to fix on one of the deeper squares of salmon pink on the wall. His voice was toneless. "Not even my brother and sister know. But for you...because you are more important to me than anything else...I will tell you what I would tell no-one else."

He paused, obviously composing his thoughts and not liking any of them. Then he drew in a quick breath. His eyes came back to her, a flat, bleak blue. His mouth curled a little as he spoke, whether in irony or self-mockery Eden couldn't tell.

"I have no child, Eden. The child conceived before my marriage was not my child. He is being brought up by his real father. So I have no place in his life."

The quiet statement of fact was like a bullet through Eden's brain, shattering all the foundations of her reasoning against accepting Luke's offer of marriage. Not for one moment did she disbelieve what he said. All the qualities of character that Luke had displayed to her had never been consistent with him abandoning a child. Why had it taken her so long to realise that?

"You knew? When you got married?" The words jerked out of her in a strangled voice.

Luke shook his head. "I was told the child was mine. I had no reason to doubt it. I didn't think of doubting it."

"But you found out?"

"After the child was born, the real father wanted custody."

"Oh, my God!" She stared at him in appalled horror as the implications of such a dreadful situation sank in. To have thought the child was his, and then to have it claimed by someone else!

His mouth twisted. "It was not the best time of my life. Diane put me through hell."

"Did you love her?" Eden asked gently. Maybe she could replace his first wife.

Luke slowly shook his head. "No. I didn't love Diane, but I liked her well enough, and I thought we could make a reasonable go of marriage. I looked forward to having a child. Afterwards..." He shrugged, but it was not a careless shrug, more an attempt to shift a bitterly heavy burden.

"Why did she do it?"

"Money. I was completely duped."

"And you thought the same thing was happening with me. The past repeating itself."

It snapped him back to the present. The blue eyes sharpened urgently on hers. "Eden, I'm so sorry..."

"It's not your fault, Luke. It's my fault. I thought you didn't want children."

He grimaced at her allusion to his attitude with her. "That was my pride speaking. Of course, I want children. I guess most men do. At least during some part of their life."

Eden nodded. It had always seemed unnatural to her that Luke didn't. As relief surged through her, bringing a trembling weakness to her legs, she sank down on her chair again. "So what happened with Diane?" she prompted softly.

He heaved a deep sigh but he still looked tense. He did not sit down. One hand gripped the back rest of his chair, his knuckles showing white. He made a dismissive gesture with his other hand. "I excused most things that happened between us because of her pregnancy."

His eyes swept Eden's in understanding concern. "I appreciate that it's not an easy time. I was as supportive of Diane as I could be, looking after her, going to prenatal classes with her. I really looked forward to the birth of the baby. And I felt once we had the child, things would be better between us."

His gaze dropped from hers. He stared at his hand gripping the chair. He relaxed his fingers, trailed them across the wood. "I was with her at the birth. It was a worry at the time because I thought the baby was about three weeks premature. But everything went okay. To me it was...a very magic moment. Unforgettable." He dragged the words out in a low, strained voice. "When that newborn baby, whom I thought was my son, was laid in my arms..."

He shook his head. His voice dropped lower. "He didn't look like me but that didn't matter. Lots of kids take more after their mother's side of the family than their father's. I thought he was mine...and I loved him."

There was a world of pain in those words. Eden remained silent. There was nothing she could say to wipe away an agony that had eaten into Luke so deeply he felt he didn't ever want to have another child.

He let go of the chair, turned away, walked slowly down the room to the bed, as though needing time to gather his composure. He sat down on the bed, leaned forward, resting his forearms on his knees. His hands rubbed at each other, fingers dragging at the skin. He flashed Eden a dark and secret smile.

"He was the light of my life for three weeks. It was worth having Diane as my wife just to have him. But then his real father turned up. Everything fell apart."

"Where had the father been?" Eden asked softly.

"Caught up in the Middle East crisis. Diane apparently decided then that I was a much better bet as a husband and father to the baby."

He gave a bitter little laugh. "She denied it all at the time. She'd got used to the good life with me, having money to spend on whatever she wanted. But you only had to look at the baby and the father to know it was his child. The same nose. The same eyes. The same ears. Well, here he had a son, a piece of life that was very precious to him."

He shrugged and tried to smile bravely at Eden. "So I gave Diane the money she wanted. I gave the father his son. And in return they gave me a promise of silence. It was not a story that I wanted running through the business world.''

It was far more than his pride that was wounded, Eden thought. Luke must have been torn apart, giving up the baby he had loved. She understood his decision never to see the child again, and her heart twisted in compassion for the loss he had suffered.

"What happened to them?" she asked.

"They eventually patched up their differences and married,'' Luke answered matter-of-factly. "The father started an engineering company. A couple of years ago they were divorced. The father got custody. I have no reason to doubt that he's a good father to his son, Eden.''

She nodded. No wonder he wanted a woman who didn't pretend. What harm had she done when she had pretended not to be pregnant? Was it irreparable?

"I'm sorry I had to ask,'' she said, painfully conscious of all he had revealed. "I'm sorry for what I did. Thank you for telling me, Luke. I'll never—''

"It's my fault, Eden,'' he cut in, the blue eyes begging her forgiveness. "I knew I wasn't being fair to you. I told you so at the time. I thought I couldn't bear to go through another marriage, another childbirth. I thought living together was better. The difference is . . . I fell in love with you. When you left . . .''

Eden's mind instantly leapt to that most wretched of moments. Her eyes searched his anxiously. "It's your child, too, Luke. If you can't believe that . . .''

"I know it's mine, Eden,'' he assured her. He stood up and walked towards her. "I know what happened. I was not really doubting you. It was more the memory of last time. Do you understand how painful that had to be?''

"Yes." She heaved a sigh of deep relief. "I couldn't have borne it if you thought..."

"I don't," he promised her.

Hope flowered between them, a beautiful, glowing hope that held so many other promises.

"Do you resent me having the baby?" Eden asked tentatively.

He took her hands, drew her up from the chair, his eyes gentle and loving as he wrapped her in his embrace. "It's our baby," he said simply.

"You don't mind too much?"

"Are you lonely, Eden?"

"Desperately lonely."

"So am I."

"Can you bear going through another childbirth with me, Luke?" Her heart was pounding fit to burst.

"That's what we're going to do, Eden," he answered softly. "For us to be together... in everything."

As her tightly held breath rushed out, she sagged against the wonderful warmth and strength of him and lifted her hands to link around his neck. Her black eyes shone with all that she felt for him. "I love you, Luke," she said simply.

He gathered her closer. So close she could feel his heartbeat echoing hers. "Does that mean we're going to get married, Eden?"

"If you ask me..."

"I'm asking you to marry me."

All the lost dreams for her future came shimmering back in glorious colour. "Yes, I will. I want that. I want that... very much."

His chest heaved against her tender breasts. Slowly, very slowly, he lowered his head to hers. Their mouths met in a beautiful sealing of their love for each other.

Paradise regained, Eden thought with dizzying pleasure. But not a limited paradise this time. There were no limits at all.

Relief and happiness gradually melted into a passion for more closeness. Luke reluctantly ended the intimacy of one long kiss and murmured, "Come home with me, Eden. I need you beside me. I want to wake in the morning and find you there with me. We can come back tomorrow and pack your things."

"Yes," she breathed ecstatically.

Eden was locking the door of her room behind them when she remembered Marlee. If it wasn't for Marlee, none of this would have happened. She would still be alone and miserable and looking at a dark future instead of what she had now.

She looked at the man she loved with all her mind and heart and soul, appealing for his understanding and patience. "Luke, I've got to call Marlee first. I'll explain to you later. It is important. Do you mind?"

He smiled. "Go right ahead. I've a lot of time for Marlee."

The truest friend any person ever had, Eden thought, ashamed that she had let her down. She hurried to the phone in the kitchen, Luke trailing after her, not wanting to let her out of his sight. As she fished the right coins out of her handbag and pushed them into the slot, her heart twisted at the grief she had unwittingly given Marlee. That had to be ended without any further delay.

However, it was her husband who answered the call.

"It's Eden, Ray. Could I please speak to Marlee?" she asked quickly.

There was a pause. A heavy sigh. "I'm sorry, Eden. Marlee is . . . she's . . . She's very distressed."

Eden felt wretchedly guilty for what she had done. "I'm sorry, Ray. Will you please tell her that I'm with Luke? And that we're going to be married. And I thank her with all my heart for—"

"Hold it!" Ray snapped, his voice suddenly sharp with new life. "You're with Luke?"

"Yes."

"And you're going to marry him?"

"Yes."

"Hang on, Eden. I think Marlee might want to change her mind and talk to you after all."

Another pause, rent with nervous urgency. Then Marlee on the line, her voice quavering with the need to believe. "Eden? Are you really with Luke?"

"Yes, Marlee. Do you want to speak to him? He's right next to me. He's waiting to take me home with him," Eden assured her, her own voice husky with emotion.

"Oh, Eden!" Marlee burst into tears. "I didn't want to do what I did," she sobbed. "But I had to. Because I love you. I... I thought I'd lost you, that we'd all lost you..." She couldn't go on.

Eden was moved to tears, as well. "You'll never lose me, Marlee. Thank you, my dearest friend, my true sister. I love you, too. More than I can ever say."

"You'll forgive me, Eden?" Marlee managed with difficulty.

"There's nothing to forgive. You had to make me see..."

"Our dreams..." Marlee choked out.

"You made them come true, Marlee."

"You made them for me, Eden. Without you..."

"Without you I would be bereft of everything. I'm going home with Luke now, Marlee."

"Home. We made it, didn't we, Eden? We made it together."

"Yes. We made it."

"Sweet dreams, Eden."

It was what they used to say to each other in the dark at the welfare home, to ward off the miserable reality of their lives.

"Sweet dreams, Marlee," Eden answered huskily.

She hung up the telephone and turned to the man she loved, the brother of the man Marlee loved. Her black eyes glittered with emotion too deep to speak.

"Will you take me home, Luke?" was all she could say.

He scooped her up in his arms and carried her to his car, hugging her all the way.

CHAPTER FOURTEEN

EDEN FINISHED preparing the salad and washed her hands at the kitchen sink. She looked out the window to where Luke was preparing the barbecue. Their visitors would be arriving any minute; Luke's sister, Pam, and her family; Marlee and Ray and their darling little daughter, Amanda; Kate Reid and her new fiancé, Trevor Anders.

It was a beautiful day, the sky as blue and as brilliantly sunny as on Marlee's wedding day, which was almost three years ago now. Eden smiled as Luke crouched down to talk to their son. David's little face was screwed up in concern as he pointed to their beloved dog who was rooting around the shrubs near the magnolia tree. Luke shook his head and yelled for Goldie to get out of the garden.

Her garden. Eden laughed to herself. Luke had declared that every boy should have a dog, and he and David had sworn that no harm would come to any of Eden's precious plants. She didn't really mind if it did. She had so much garden—exactly as she wanted it— that a little damage now and then was well and truly compensated by the pleasure Luke and David had in the labrador pup they had chosen together.

Goldie shot to them, his tail wagging like mad. David hugged him. Luke gave him an affectionate scratch behind one ear. So much for scolding, Eden thought in amusement. Although she had to admit that she herself was hopelessly indulgent towards the pup's antics.

She turned off the tap, dried her hands, then stepped out onto the veranda. She paused to look up at the graceful white aluminium lace that decorated the eaves and each veranda post. She loved everything about this house, even to the creaky step in the staircase that led up to the bedroom floor.

Luke saw her and waved her out to join him. David came pelting towards her with Goldie skipping delightedly around his heels. "Nothing got hurt in the garden, Mummy," he assured her as he curled his little hand around hers and started dragging her with him to the barbecue area.

Eden laughed. David was so beautiful, so endearing in his ways, and so very like Luke. His eyes were as blue as today's sky. Eden wondered if their next child would have black eyes like her.

"I guess that has to be a new creation of Kate's," Luke called out, his eyes running over her in dancing appreciation.

"Of course," she replied with a broad grin. Eden knew she looked good. The cleverly cut pink slacks and overblouse were designed to make a six-months-pregnant mother look good. Kate's Maternity in Bloom line was selling like hot cakes.

"I'll have to congratulate her again," Luke said, returning Eden's grin.

His bank's investment in Kate Reid's fashion business was really paying off. Eden was delighted that she had been able to help Kate develop and sell her talent. Slum kids had to stick together in order to get ahead in this life, she thought with satisfaction.

Eden bought all her clothes from Kate now, much to Paula Michaelson's pique. Eden didn't feel she owed Paula anything. But for Luke, the Staffords would have wiped their hands of her. Money didn't buy real friendship. Nor did it buy love.

"Mind you," Luke said, sliding his arm around her shoulders and hugging her to his side, "you would look beautiful to me no matter what you wore."

She looked up at him, loving him for all that he was. "Or if I wore nothing at all?" she teased.

He tenderly caressed the slight bulge under her blouse. "Especially with nothing at all," he answered, blue eyes dancing wickedly. "Any movement from our daughter today?"

They already knew the sex of their unborn baby from an ultra-scan, and they were both delighted at the prospect of having a little sister for David. "I think she might be resting after last night," Eden said, her black eyes twinkling with the same happy wickedness.

"Mmm... Have I told you lately how much I love you?"

Luke's love for her was all around Eden ... the beautiful home he had bought her, the glorious garden he had helped her to create, the son he had given her, the daughter in her womb, the gold wedding ring on her finger, the embrace in which he held her, the wonderful life he had made possible for her.

"I love you," she said with all her heart.

He smiled. "That's because we're good together."

"Yes. It's because we're good together," Eden repeated happily.

No risks, no prizes...

The words drifted through her mind. They didn't really apply any more, she thought. She had all the prizes.

WORDFIND #7

```
F A T H E R H O O D F G B E
M A A S R F I B C M O K T Y D
A A C B V Z S C N D G J K O E
A C R X B K S M T O H G K D N
Q W E R B S E H R K M J D A P
U S D A I G H N E R V M C I O
L K D F B A N E M E Y U Y O S
P W E R T Y Y W I O H P L F H
H R G E K Y W L E T D Y O P P
V B I J K B L U K O M F D H K
W G Z Z T L E E R E N I B O L
A S D F E E G R U V B P N M
N X D F Y S N D U X H J L
A N A D V E N T U R H B
```

ADVENTURE   MARRIAGE
DARCY   MOTHERHOOD
EDEN   PRIZES
EMMA   RISKS
FATHERHOOD   SELBY
LUKE   SYDNEY

**Look for A YEAR DOWN UNDER Wordfind #8
in August's Harlequin Presents #1577
THE STONE PRINCESS by Robyn Donald**   WF7

Discover the glorious triumph of three
extraordinary couples fueled by a powerful
passion to defy the past in

The dramatic story of six fascinating men and
women who find the strength to step out of the
shadows and into the light of a passionate future.

Linked by relentless ambition and by desire, each
must confront private demons in a riveting struggle
for power. Together they must find the strength to
emerge from the lingering shadows of the past, into
the dawning promise of the future.

Look for this powerful new blockbuster by *New
York Times* bestselling author

Available in August at your favorite retail outlet.
PJLS93

WHEN STOLEN MOMENTS
ARE ALL YOU HAVE...

The sun is hot and you've got a few minutes
to catch some rays....

And what better way to spend the time than with
SUMMER MADNESS—our summer promotion that features
six new individual short contemporary stories.

SIZZLE	Jennifer Crusie
ANNIVERSARY WALTZ	Anne Marie Duquette
MAGGIE AND HER COLONEL	Merline Lovelace
PRAIRIE SUMMER	Alina Roberts
THE SUGAR CUP	Annie Sims
LOVE ME NOT	Barbara Stewart

Each story is a complete romance that's just the perfect length
for the busy woman of the nineties... but still providing the
perfect blend of adventure, sensuality and, of course, romance!

Look for the special displays in July and share some of the
Summer Madness!

HSM-1

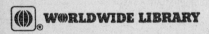

WORLDWIDE LIBRARY

Harlequin is proud to present our best authors and their best books. Always the best for your reading pleasure!

Throughout 1993, Harlequin will bring you exciting books by some of the top names in contemporary romance!

In July
look for
The Ties That Bind by JAYNE ANN KRENTZ

Shannon wanted him seven days a week....

Dark, compelling, mysterious Garth Sheridan was no mere boy next door—even if he did rent the cottage beside Shannon Raine's.

She was intrigued by the hard-nosed exec, but for Shannon it was all or nothing. Either break the undeniable bonds between them... or tear down the barriers surrounding Garth and discover the truth.

Don't miss THE TIES THAT BIND ...
wherever Harlequin books are sold.

BOB3

HARLEQUIN ✦ PRESENTS®

A Year
DOWN UNDER

In 1993, Harlequin Presents celebrates the land down
under. In August, let us take you to Auckland and
Northland, New Zealand, in THE STONE PRINCESS by
Robyn Donald, Harlequin Presents #1577.

They'd parted eight years ago, but Petra still feels
something for Caine Fleming. Now the handsome New
Zealander wants to reconcile, but Petra isn't convinced of
his true feelings for her. She does know that she wants—
that she *needs*—any reconciliation to be more than a
marriage of convenience. Petra wants Caine body and soul.

Share the adventure—and the romance—of
A Year Down Under!

Available wherever Harlequin books are sold.

SOLUTIONS TO
WORDFIND #7